The Bride of Northanger

A *Jane Austen* Variation

by

Diana Birchall

White Soup Press

The Bride of Northanger: A Jane Austen Variation
Copyright © 2019 by Diana Birchall
Published by White Soup Press
All rights reserved, including the right to reproduce this book, or portions thereof, in any format whatsoever.

To my dear friend and correspondent
Janet Todd,
who wrote, and practices,
"Women's Friendship in Literature"
– and in life.

I could a tale unfold, whose lightest word
Would harrow up thy soul.

- Shakespeare (*Hamlet)*

Chapter One

If Catherine Morland was not born to be a heroine, she ended by becoming something very like one. In the first place, heroine-like, she was so fortunate as to marry the man of her choice at the age of only eighteen. Henry Tilney was, her parents knew, beyond her deserts in a worldly way, for he was the second son of General Tilney, whose fine landed estate and seat at Northanger Abbey entitled him to a voice in the affairs of the nation. To say the truth, Henry was rather a disappointment to his father's vanity, for he had not the ambition General Tilney desired to see in him; he neither wished to amass a great fortune of his own, nor to be a fashionable figure at court nor a practiced politician. Henry was a clergyman, established in a comfortable family living at Woodston Rectory; and he asked nothing better.

A particular point of disagreement with his father, was that Henry considered as indispensible to his happiness, the blessing of choosing for himself a thoroughly amiable wife. His settling on Catherine, young and unformed, of no very distinguished lineage, and with only three thousand pounds, had brought down the wrath of the General; wrath all the more violent because of himself having initially promoted the marriage, under a mistaken idea that Catherine was an heiress. On discovering otherwise, he had shockingly turned his young guest out of Northanger Abbey, so that she was forced to travel home alone, a journey of seventy miles, exposed to all the dangers and discomforts of hackney-coaches.

Henry was ordered to give her up; but having engaged her faith, he stood firm, and for the first time in his life refused to obey his father. The young people were obliged to wait for their happiness, but time, and persuasion, had done the business. Now they were married; and a happier heroine than young Mrs. Tilney did not exist in England.

The evening before the wedding, Henry slept at the Fullerton rectory, Catherine's home, so that they might have an early start to their journey on the wedding-morning.

Despite his happiness, he seemed preoccupied, and at last, with some seriousness, told Catherine that he wished to have a word with her and her mother and father, before retiring for the night. Though somewhat surprised, Catherine helped get the younger children off to bed, and then joined Mr. and Mrs. Morland and Henry in her father's study.

"What have you to say, Mr. Tilney?" said Mrs. Moreland, good humouredly. "Sure, you need not ask for Catherine's hand again? Every thing is nicely settled in that way, and we are in full readiness for tomorrow, though here I am, still whipping up this last bit of lace for Catherine's wedding-dress. You are a sad girl, to be sure, leaving it for me to do."

"No – Mr. and Mrs. Morland, it is something else, that must be said, though I am very sorry to have waited for so long. I ought to have spoken sooner."

Catherine was alarmed. "It is not something to do with your father again?" she cried. "Oh, no, Henry!"

"No, it is not that at all – only that it does have something to do with him, in a way," Henry stopped in confusion, and the Morlands looked at him with surprise, as he was usually readiness with words itself.

"Only speak your mind, my boy," said Mr. Morland kindly; "I am sure it can be nothing so very bad."

"It is indeed nothing, in truth, a nonsense, a foolishness. And yet, it is right that you should know. I have not spoken of this until now, because my dearest Catherine, with all her good will, is a person of such real imagination - and so fond as she is of the novels of Mrs. Radcliffe and her sensational sisters - that I feared she might be frightened by what I have to say," he finished, not very coherently.

"I know what you mean," said her mother, with a sage nod. "That bad habit of hers, of reading immoderately. That was what did the business, I am sure. She has been silly enough; but she is mended now, and grown quite a sensible girl I assure you, not much given to frights."

Catherine's eyes were fixed on Henry's agitated expression. "For Heaven's sake, Henry, what is it?" she asked.

"Yes, you had much better speak out, Mr. Tilney," said Mr. Morland, firmly.

"It is only this. I have never told you – you have not heard – "

"What is it?" exclaimed three voices, and Henry resolutely spoke.

"That - that there is a curse upon Northanger Abbey!"

There was a small silence, and then his three listeners burst into laughter.

"You had me fooled for an instant," said Mr. Morland, "A very good joke, to be sure. Perhaps a trifle too alarming for the ladies, however. And in my opinion, the night before your wedding ought not to be the occasion for such pleasantries, if I may be allowed to say so. But there's no harm done."

"Indeed, Mr. Tilney," nodded Mrs. Morland, "you gave me quite a start. Curses, indeed! That is not my idea of wit, but when Catherine has you all to herself at Woodston, you will amuse one another sure enough."

"Oh, yes," said Catherine, fondly. "Henry's wit is my delight. I daresay he is trying to frighten me now, but it is all in fun."

Henry looked at her with concern. "Catherine, my dear – Mr. and Mrs. Morland – please do not misunderstand me. It is not a joke. What you are kind enough to call my wit, I hope would be regulated by taste, and a fit sense of the occasion. Be assured, I would not make a jest of this nature."

"Tell me another story, Mr. Tilney. You are a sad joker for a son-in-law," said Mrs. Morland, shaking her head and taking up her lace again.

"My dear ma'am – how can I convince you, that what I say is true enough? There *is* a curse upon the Abbey."

Mr. Morland's voice reflected his disapproval. "What nonsense, my boy. I must say I am surprised to hear you speak in this way. And you a man of the cloth! Why would you choose to harrow up our spirits with such a tale?"

"And at such a time, too," reminded Mrs. Morland reprovingly.

"Truly a curse?" cried Catherine. "Oh, what is it? But of course it cannot be true."

"Certainly it is not true, my dear," said her father firmly, "there are no such things as curses. I am afraid Mr. Tilney is being facetious; but if he is not, then I hope to hear a sincere explanation directly."

"I do not know how to speak of this, in such a way as to make you understand," said Henry earnestly. "I would not wish to speak in an overwrought manner, or be guilty of using exaggerated language. No, sir, you are quite justified in opposing the idea of curses; I do not believe in them either. That would neither be rational nor right, for one who has taken the Church as his profession."

"I am thankful to hear you say so, Mr. Tilney," said Mr. Morland, relieved. "Do I collect, then, that there is some tradition of the sort in your family? In that case, I can appreciate your reluctance to expose Catherine to tales that are both dreadful and baseless."

"Yes," said Mrs. Moreland, "she has been such a fanciful young creature, ten to one she might have thought it was true, and got a fright. But I do believe that Catherine is much more common-sensical than she used to be. She has quite given over reading those horrid novels, though I never have been able to make her attend to good Miss Edgeworth's tales."

"Those are for children, Mother," protested Catherine. "You know that Henry and I have done a great deal of serious reading together, since we have been engaged, of a philosophical and scientific nature; and Rousseau and Linnaeus are far more interesting to me now."

Mrs. Morland looked uneasy. "You will become quite a learned lady, Catherine," she said.

This made Henry smile in spite of himself. "Do not fear that, Mrs. Morland," he assured her. "I thought a little instruction in the enlightened thinking of our age, would be of benefit to Catherine, but no more than *that*."

He probably thought that to live in the country year round with a wife whose mind had been sadly unfurnished by parents too occupied with raising a family of ten children, might lose its charms; and while Catherine did not threaten to become a bluestocking, she had, in the year of their engagement, duly devoured some very wise books indeed.

"On reflection, I believe you did right in telling us of this story," pursued Mr. Morland, "as Catherine might hear it elsewhere, and be distressed. Yes, she had best hear it from you. But what sort of tale is this, pray? Is it a very old one?"

"Yes, it has been handed down in my family for many generations," said Henry seriously.

"Has it indeed? Come, then, tell us all, unless you would rather relate it to me first, and then judge about telling Catherine and her mother."

"What would be the use of that?" asked Mrs. Morland, practically. "The cat is already out of the bag, and it can hardly be as bad as what Catherine could scare herself with."

"True; and it is essential that Catherine must know, before we are married."

Catherine went to him, and took his arm. "Tell me all about it now, Henry," she said as calmly as possible.

"It is this. Northanger Abbey, as you know, was once a monastic institution. Its grounds were consecrated for the better part of a thousand years."

"When I was a silly girl," said Catherine with a faint smile, "last year, you remember how I hoped it would have a regularly horrid history, and was disappointed to find the place had so modern an appearance."

"It is only the bones of the actual Gothic building that remain intact," Henry reminded her, "the stone walls and arches, with the quadrangle now only partly enclosed by the old convent. It is a matter of regret that the Abbey itself was despoiled at the time of King Henry VIII. The Tilney of that generation, the first Frederick, was one of Cromwell's men, and his depredations were terrible. He sacked the Abbey, hanged the Abbot, and slaughtered the poor monks."

"Oh! I hate to hear that story," Catherine shuddered. "It is so very dreadful, indeed, that it almost makes me not want to go near the place again."

"I am sorry you should feel so," said Henry soberly, "but now I must tell you the rest. When the Abbot was dying – a great and saintly man he was, Father Abbot Stephen - he called down a curse on Tilney and all his heirs, in perpetuity, in God's name. His voice was uncannily carried all over the country side, so that every body heard it; as though he was yahooing through a horn."

The Morlands looked appalled. "And what," faltered Catherine, "what was the curse?"

"'That the race of Tilney might survive, but its fruitfulness be blighted forevermore. The wife of each firstborn son would die, either in terror or in madness, early in her life, and long before her appointed time."

"Oh no!" cried Mrs. Morland, her hand to her mouth, "surely this must be a terrible joke, after all! For otherwise, who would marry into such a family?" She stopped, in horrified realization of what she had said.

"Stay," said Mr. Morland, coolly. "You forget that Henry is not a firstborn son. The curse – not that there is such a thing, naturally – cannot be held to apply to him and his wife."

"That is true," said Henry, looking anxiously at Catherine. "There is no malevolent imprecation against second sons, and in any case, as you truly say, sir, it is nothing but an old superstition. However, servants and country people do tell wild tales; and that is why I knew I must tell Catherine before my family was hers. Can you forgive me, my Catherine, now that you know all?"

Catherine met his eyes with a reassuring smile.

"Oh, yes. It must have been hard for you to tell me. But you have taught me to be rational, Henry. It is only a Chimaera, I know."

"A what?" asked Mrs. Morland.

"A Chimaera," said Catherine with a look at her mother that was a touch pitying, "is a fire-breathing, female monster, composed of many animal parts put together."

"Catherine, I beg to know what you mean by that."

"Why, I mean only that it is an impossible fantasy, Mother. Henry has been making me read Homer. Only in translation, of course, but that is owing to the deficiencies of a female education."

"Chimaeras and curses – Heaven on earth! Catherine, how can you! And I don't know what is all this fine talk of education. We never could get learning to stick to you, before this."

"All I mean to say, Ma'am," said Catherine, with proper deference, "is, that I shall endeavor not to give this story another thought."

"Quite right, my dear," said her father. "Though I suppose we had better know all. Have there, in sober fact, been sufficient untimely deaths among the Tilney wives, to give weight to the story, among the credulous?"

"Yes," said Henry reluctantly, "I must say there have."

"Your own mother," Catherine said with compunction, remembering her own dreadful conjectures about poor Mrs. Tilney, the most lurid of which had been that the poor woman had been walled up alive.

"Yes, my mother did die of a short and painful illness," he said slowly, "and my grandmother, my father's mother, died early, too, in childbed, giving birth to my father."

"So he was motherless," Catherine reflected. "No wonder, then, that he grew up to be so – not pleasant. He is a most unhappy man."

"Why Catherine," said her mother, "that's not in reason. Many people lose their mothers, and it does not follow that they turn out ill-tempered, or have any untoward qualities. Ten to one the General's temperament is natural with him."

"And farther back than your grandmother?" Mr. Morland pressed, curiously.

"Yes – there are legends. I do not know them all. My sister Eleanor does; her nurse would tell them to her. There is a positively ghastly gallery of beheadings and fatal falls and swift illnesses. I am sure you need not hear a recitation, even if I were able to give you a catalogue of them."

"No; rather not," said Mr. Morland. "Indeed, I think, now that you have disburthened yourself, that the best thing we can do, is to try to forget the story. It is only a pity you did not tell it earlier, so as not to make a shadow over Catherine's last night at home."

"I really could not bring myself to speak before," Henry confessed. "The distressing and the absurd are so unfortunately blended, and the place has a most sordid history. Even the good monks themselves were – not so good."

"What did they do?" Catherine asked curiously.

"Well – you have heard of the Holy Blood that was kept in a chalice, and how pilgrims from all over the land came to worship this relic? The practice was even known to Chaucer, who wrote about it."

Mr. Morland said nothing, and his wife only shook her head.

"The so-called Holy Blood proved to be nothing but a money making scheme. Only those of pure conscience were supposed able to see the blood, but after they had paid, and prayed, most penitents could see it."

"Is that really true, Henry?" breathed Catherine.

"The blood was found to be that of ducks," he told her with a droll look, "easily renewable, and the chalice had two sides, one with blood showing, and the other painted black. The monks made a fortune."

"I thought you said that Abbot was saintly."

"He was a good man; and he did not start these practices."

"It was such abuses that led to the dissolution of the monasteries," Mr. Morland observed.

"So you see, the history of my house, and my family, is altogether a lurid recitation; though the curse is the tale we naturally find most unsettling. Perhaps you can understand my reluctance to talk, or even think about it."

"I don't blame you," said Mrs. Morland candidly. "No one likes to tell any thing shocking of their family, and your story is enough to give me quite a turn. However, I trust that, with all her fine reading, Catherine will not be such a simpleton as to let it worry or vex her. It is not as if you were to live at Northanger Abbey yourselves."

Catherine spoke with composure. "Oh, no. And if we ever do visit the Abbey again, Henry, depend upon it I shall be quite inured to its terrible history."

"That is sensible, my dear," her father approved.

"And you will show me the ancient portions that I have never properly seen yet, where it is all supposed to have happened. Are the monks' cells still there, I wonder – real monks? Can we see them?"

She brightened at the idea.

"The parts where the – massacre happened, were all burnt," Henry informed her, "the cells are gone, and only some of the old walls and archways are original. One side of the Abbey was so ruinous it had to be cleared entirely. You know how extensively my father has improved the interior, and how proud he is that it is not outwardly a patched-together business. It was his concern to bring modern comforts to Northanger, and in this task he has succeeded, to give him his due."

"He has. Much as I foolishly wished it, I did not see anything horrid, when I was there," she paused, without adding her private thought, "Except your father."

"You must always be careful what you wish for, my dear," her mother nodded wisely.

"I would never wish for horrors now," Catherine assured her. "But if a real massacre occurred, there might be some relics or shards of fossilized bone left," she speculated, with something of her old interest.

"You won't find any such things at Woodston, you know," Henry reminded her with an arch smile.

Catherine brightened. "Oh, Woodston is the most comfortable, the loveliest place in the world! And we are going there tomorrow," she said, recalled to her proper state of bridal rapture.

"Yes, tomorrow," said Henry, and they smiled at each other.

"And you will be tired tomorrow, unless we all get to bed. It is nearly ten o'clock," said Mrs. Morland briskly. "James, will you get the candles ready, while I put away my work."

Chapter Two

The wedding was not one that would have made a show according to the General's ideas; but his approval of the quiet ceremony and homely refreshment afterwards, was not required, for he was happily not among those present. The bride's father read the service with proper emotion in his voice, and after a light collation, and the considerable business of being kissed by all her numerous brothers and sisters, the bride and groom were duly seated in his carriage, she in her new bridal finery and he in the very same handsomely caped greatcoat that she had first admired. And so they drove away, among many good natured cries wishing them good health and good luck.

Once before, Catherine had journeyed on this road, alone and miserable, exiled from Northanger Abbey by her present father-in-law; but on this occasion, with what entirely different feelings did she seat herself in Henry's curricle, and rejoice in the smart equipage, as the pretty, fast-stepping horses made good speed on the road toward what she already gladly thought of as home. Even the fleeting thought of the family curse, that would intrude, gave only an exciting fillip to her happy spirits.

It was a journey of fifty miles, for Woodston was twenty miles closer to Fullerton than Northanger; but with only a rest at Salisbury, and stopping for some cold victuals at Marlborough, the young couple crossed into Gloucestershire and reached Woodston village after a journey of not more than seven hours, long before they could tire of being on the road, or of being in each other's company.

All good things, as her mother was fond of saying, come to an end, however, and so Catherine alighted from the carriage with a spring, as fresh and as gay as she had started out in the morning, and after turning the horses over to his groom, Henry, with feelings of the greatest gladness, invited his bride into her new home.

Catherine had seen Woodston before, but now there was all the fresh delight of discovering every thing Henry had done to the place, to prepare it for her reception. Her conviction, from her only previous visit, that it was the most delightful of all houses in the world, was swiftly confirmed.

The servants welcomed her warmly, and she was shown to her freshly decorated, pretty chamber, where her new maid, Annette, the young niece of the housekeeper, and very happy and important in her new position, helped her to change her dress. Still not at all fatigued, Catherine stepped outside into the grounds, where Henry was waiting for her, accompanied by his dogs.

"Oh! How the little terrier puppies are grown," she cried.

"That is in the natural course of things, as you last saw them a year ago," Henry told her with a smile.

"How I do love them," she exulted, kneeling down. "I might say I married you for their sake, only I don't want to make you jealous."

"Jealous of Archimedes and Artemis?" Henry pretended outrage.

"Not of their names, at any rate," Catherine amended.

After fifteen minutes' romp on the grass, Henry looked at the sky, as if pleased with every thing that was under it. "My housekeeper, Mrs. Billings – our housekeeper, I mean - hinted at some fine preparations going on for our supper. Perhaps we had better go in and pretend surprise."

As they passed into the house, Catherine paused for another rapturous look at the drawing-room, that she had thought perfection, even before there was a stick of furniture in it. Last year there had been nothing to be seen but polished floors and long windows looking out onto the green meadows; but Henry, with some advice and assistance from his sister, had fitted it up charmingly. Two low seats by the fire looked particularly inviting, and Henry pointed out the well-filled book case nearby.

"Here are Cowper, and Crabbe, and Scott," he said enthusiastically, "and we will read poetry together, and some science, this winter – I have some mind to build an orrery."

"Will we? How delightful! Is it a bird-cage?"

"No, my love, a thing to trace the stars."

His cheek was close to hers, but after a few moments Catherine's attention was distracted by the entrancing wall-paper, in a pretty pattern with Chinese birds and flowers.

"Why! Those are hyacinths!"

"Eleanor sent for the paper from Paris," Henry explained, "to commemorate how first you learned to love a hyacinth, and then, myself – or at least, my dogs."

"Our dogs," Catherine reminded him, "though I hope to claim the privilege of my new married state, and have the naming of the next litter myself."

"You shall do all the naming in this family," promised Henry, raising a faint blush in Catherine.

Henry next took his lady in to the dining-room, where roasted spring lamb and green peas were brought in, followed by strawberries and a large white cake that the cook had prepared in their honour. Glasses of wine were poured out as they sat by the fire, and read their first poem together. It was not a long one, only an extract from the Lyrical Ballads.

"The eye it cannot chuse but see,
"We cannot bid the ear be still;
"Our bodies feel, where'er they be,
"Against, or with our will.

After reading it, Henry, his eyes demurely lowered, proposed an early retiring.

He took up his candle, and showed Catherine to her room, where the maid waited to comb out her hair. At just the proper moment he returned, to make what he must have felt a daring proposal: that instead of setting up rooms of their own, they should sleep altogether in hers, and his be used only as a dressing-room and to keep some of his papers and books.

This seemed to Catherine only a very sensible and natural proposal, for it was no more than what her parents had always done, though she could not look at him as she agreed to it; and so they retired to bed, and together blew out the candles.

Chapter Three

The dogs' barking outside awoke Mrs. Henry Tilney, and she opened her eyes just at the moment her new husband opened his.

"How do you do, my Catherine?" he asked tenderly.

"Oh, I am very well. But I always am in the morning."

"But this is a different sort of morning," he reminded her archly, "the very first of our married life."

She was lost in joyful contemplation of the doubtless unending succession of mornings that they would welcome together in perfect joy. As Henry then asked her what she thought of it, the answer required some explanation, which Henry then elaborated upon so eloquently that Catherine wished he might never stop. But upon their noticing with surprise that the sun was rising in the sky, much faster than it ever had been seen to do before, Henry considerately retired to his own room to prepare for the day, saying that he would send the maid to her, with a cup of chocolate.

The forenoon was spent in making a circuit of the parish. Henry introduced his bride to the parishioners and cottagers, all of whom made very much of her; and afterwards they retired to a survey of their own grounds, projecting plantings, and visiting the animals.

"It is the happiest day I ever spent," Catherine declared, as they sat down to tea at their own table, spread with their own new china set, General Tilney's wedding-present, which Catherine had not before seen.

He was a connoisseur in china, as in many other things, and Catherine could not but admire the delicate gold-and-white dishes and cups, in their prettiness and abundance, however empty was the sentiment behind the sending.

"Happiness is a very proper state in a new bride," observed Henry, "and I may take the opportunity to tell you that I am happy, too. Upon my word, my father did us well! That is a set that might last us all our lives, even if we have as large a family as yours."

Catherine blushed again at this reference, and then felt it ungracious to have a secret hope that using the china would not always make her think of the giver.

"The gold leaves are very pretty," she said, taking up a cup. "I never saw any thing like these little symbols woven round the edges. Do they signify any thing, do you think?"

"I do not know. I had not observed," said Henry, examining a saucer closely. "You are right, however, they look almost like letters, do they not?"

"Not in any language I ever saw. Is it Russian? Is it Hebrew? Is it Arabic?"

Henry squinted at length, and finally said, "No. I perceive they are English letters, but they are so very small, I do not think they can possibly be read without a magnification glass. We have not one here. I should have to send to Cambridge for such a thing."

"Well, I wish you would. If there is some secret writing on our china, I should like to know what it says. Do you think your father knows about it?"

"Most certainly. My father does nothing without deliberation. And he had this china made up especially for you –he told me so, in the letter that accompanied it. I can't comprehend what he means by this."

"Perhaps the letters are a motto of some sort," suggested Catherine. "My mother has a set of plates that have a blessing on them, and the words, *Hunger is the Best Sauce.*"

"Somehow I feel it is not that," said Henry dryly.

The eyes of the young husband and wife met.

"'Tis very strange," said Catherine. "Are you quite sure you cannot make out any words at all? I could not, but then I only know English."

"It does not look like any thing else," said Henry doubtfully, "it might be Latin, but so tiny…Does this look like the letter T to you?"

"Not very much – oh, yes, perhaps it might."

"I think it is English. T, C, I…something…L, A, M, I believe, only the size of pinpoints."

"But that does not mean any thing, Henry."

"I cannot tell," he said slowly, "but I think the letters may be written backwards. Then it could be – Maledict. No, surely not. I cannot make out any more."

He put the saucer down, rather hard.

"That does not sound much like a blessing," Catherine faltered.

The young couple sat silent, as they each thought of what the words might mean, and what was the opposite of a blessing.

"I suppose I must write to thank your father," said Catherine reluctantly, "but Henry, I hope you will not take it amiss if I say I prefer not to use this set of china."

"No, I'd like to break every piece," he said savagely.

"Goodness, how glad I am that we need not make our home at Northanger," she said, low.

He looked as if he understood and fully participated in the sentiment. "No," he said, "even though my father seems to have forgiven me, in a fashion, it is a fashion of his own. Whether a greeting is intended with this china or not, I confess I do not sense friendly feeling breathing from it."

Catherine felt exactly the same and could not suppress a shudder.

"Whatever his message *says*, it is plain that its meaning is that he has no need for us," said Henry decidedly. "Which happens to coincide with my own inclinations extremely well."

"So we shall remain here?" asked Catherine hopefully.

"I wish we might, but a wedding-visit is indispensible. It will be remarked in the neighborhood, and my father cares about how things appear to – You understand. But we shall wait until Eleanor and Charles pay their next visit. My father is greedy of visits from the Viscountess, and my sister is generous in indulging him. You know what Eleanor's kindness is."

"Oh, yes," said Catherine, relieved, "and I am curious to see the Viscount."

"I think I can assure you that you will like Charles very much," said Henry with a smile. "Eleanor quite rightly thinks he is the most charming man in the world; but I suspect that is partly because he is so very different from my father."

"I confess that I can understand her reasoning," Catherine admitted.

"Charles is a particularly gentle person, softly spoken, with a fine understanding," he continued. "He is a naturalist, knows everything about birds, and grasses, and is most obliging about teaching others. We should learn much from him. Botany is a very fascinating study."

"More lessons?" inquired Catherine. "I did not know it was your plan to keep me in the school-room, Henry."

"Am I so very tiresome in my pedagogical tendencies?" said Henry with compunction.

"Not at all," she assured him. "I should hate to be a disagreeable companion through ignorance, and I hope you have found me somewhat improved, now that I have read Milton, and Johnson."

Henry laughed, and caressed her. "A man who thinks he knows it all, is invariably drawn to a woman whom he thinks knows nothing," he said, half apologetically, "and now I have shown myself to be the ignorant one, by my carelessness of your feelings. Indeed, Catherine, you are in a fair way to be a most clever, well informed woman, and by the time we are old, you will be more than a match for me."

"Well," said Catherine, not wanting to argue, "I only wonder why, when we find perfect happiness, we want immediately to change it."

Henry shook his head. "I will live to rue the day that I ever exposed you to the philosophers, and you become a very Xantippe."

"Do you mean to say that I am a shrew, and that you rank yourself with Socrates? That will not quite do, Henry!"

Henry gave her a look of mock alarm. "What have I wrought, I wonder?"

"A wife to your own taste, and of your own mind, I hope," Catherine replied. "Seriously, learning botany from our new brother-in-law will be something pleasant to do when we are at Northanger, at least."

"Much better for us to be there at the same time as Eleanor and Charles. I wish that your unhappy memories of the place, and those old stories, could all be forgotten."

"Don't worry about that. My memories are nothing, and I assure you I have no more superstitious fancies, and care nothing for curses."

Henry looked at her quizzically.

"To say the truth," she confessed, "the only thing I am still afraid of is the General. He seems to me a Malediction in his own person – though I ought not say such things of your father."

"You say nothing that he does not deserve," said Henry gravely. "If you never forgave him for his treatment of you, I should say you had reasons good. He deserves no charity, even from *your* warm heart. Be assured that if – if he ever treats you with anything but the utmost – "

"I daresay the visit will go well," she reassured him, "and we can ask him about the writing on the china. Perhaps he only meant it as a joke."

"My father has not much humour about him, of any kind," Henry told her dryly.

"I did not think so," Catherine admitted, under her breath.

"Never mind. We will have Eleanor and Charles to keep us company, and if Frederick is there too, my father will take little notice of us. He always got on best with him. Frederick is his favorite."

Chapter Four

In their second week of wedded happiness, the young Tilneys were lingering over breakfast when the morning post was brought in. Henry handed his wife a letter from her sister, while announcing one from his own; and she eagerly read hers with so much commentary and expostulation that she might as well have read the letter entirely aloud.

"Oh! Here is news. Sarah says that Mr. and Mrs. Allen are to take her to Bath. How kind they are! They say that, as her sister did so well, she should be given the same chance. Well, I know that if her residence at Bath lasted for a twelvemonth, she could never find another Henry. But I should not say so, as you have quite enough conceit as it is." She broke off, seeing Henry's face. "Why, what is it, Henry?"

"Eleanor and Charles are at Northanger," he said reluctantly, "and Eleanor presses us to join them."

"Oh! Is there any thing the matter?"

"No – no, she does not say so; it is that she desires our presence for Charles, who dislikes being the only gentleman in company with the General."

"Yes, I see," nodded Catherine. "I shall be ready in an hour, if you think it best, Henry. We can be there tonight."

He thanked her with a look. "You are all consideration," he said, "and it need not be a long visit."

Three hours' travel brought them thither, and after the pleasant ease of their own home, it was a shock to recollect that here was none of the informality of an arrival at Woodston. A fleet of grooms efficiently attended to the horses and carriage, and their young master and mistress were formally announced as they walked into the grand drawing-room.

General Tilney himself stood by the fire-place, where he had been holding forth and laying down the law to his daughter and her husband. Eleanor looked slightly harassed, though well and blooming otherwise; and Charles, a tall and slender young man, was abstractedly turning over a portfolio of ornithological drawings.

"There you are, Henry," said the General, in his booming voice, ignoring Catherine. "In good time. I have been telling her ladyship that I wish her to make a stay of some weeks. There are some of my very old friends coming – Lord Grey and Admiral Symonds, as well as our man in Parliament, Dunning; and besides, a select party of Pitt's men are doing me the honour of making a visit from London. Important matters are afoot, and I urgently require a hostess."

"Good afternoon, Sir," said Henry politely. "Here is my wife – your new daughter - here is Catherine."

She curtseyed, and he gave her a distant nod. "I hope you will use your influence with Eleanor, to impress upon her the importance of her remaining here. Charles is perfectly welcome, too, of course; I do not mean to suggest such a thing as parting them. My friends will be particularly charmed to meet Viscount Eastham."

"Dear Sir, I have told you we cannot stay," pleaded Eleanor. "Charles has other plans."

"Oh, well, if there are pre-engagements, that is another thing," the General said carelessly, "but you have not mentioned such, and I fail to see why you should not attend to your poor old father, when he needs you."

"Are you not expecting Frederick?" Henry asked, hoping to deflect him from the matter.

"Yes; he arrives tomorrow. But that's nothing to the case. The Minister will be very glad to see him – no one was ever better company than Frederick – but I must have Eleanor to do the honours of the table, you see."

Charles looked up from his drawings and fixed his father-in-law with a serious gaze. "I wish that it were possible to gratify you by a longer stay, sir," he said calmly, "but it is impossible for us to remain. I have just received a letter from my friend Lymington, who reports seeing a Papilio Machaon in his hedge. A very rare sort of swallowtail indeed. I had already intended to go to him, for there are buntings in his woods, and it is a rare privilege to hear him dilate on such things. The keenest observer of animals in England; I really believe no one knows more than he does about the tortoise."

General Tilney had looked baffled through most of this speech, but his expression cleared. "Ah, you mean the Earl of Lymington! Yes, yes, I quite see why you cannot offend such a man."

"It is not a matter for offense, but you see springtime is chiffchaff season," the young man explained.

"Well, if you must go, you must; but I hope you will at least allow me to keep Eleanor.

"We are not going quite yet, Father," Eleanor assured him, "we will help to welcome your visitors first, and then, as Henry and Catherine will be here, as well as Frederick, there is no possibility of any one feeling neglected."

"And the Easthams' departure," added Henry, "cannot be taken by any one as a discourtesy, as it is owing to a prior engagement."

"Oh, very well," said the General, disgruntled. "At any rate, you will stay, Henry. Your wife can pour the tea, in Eleanor's absence. It is better than nothing."

"I will be very glad," said Catherine faintly.

The General looked at her without seeing her. "I had most particularly wished to have them meet the Viscount," he said, his dark brows contracted with displeasure.

"Charles must not be disappointed about the tortoises, sir," his daughter said gently.

"Why shouldn't we invite Lymington here? My cook makes a very creditable turtle soup, if he likes the blessed things," suggested the General, reflectively.

"Lord Lymington would never consume a tortoise, and no more would I, sir," said Charles, rather heatedly.

No one answered, and Henry hazarded a change of subject.

"You are back from the Assizes, I think, Sir."

"Yes, yes. My duties lie heavy upon me," the General replied with an elaborate sigh. "You have little idea, as you two young couples disport yourselves on your honeymoon pleasures, how the affairs of the country take up my time. There is to be the hanging of a man accused of sedition; I must needs preside over this, though I prefer not to watch a fellow human in that state, twisting and choking upon the rope. My feelings are naturally fastidious."

"What malfeasance was committed?" asked Henry, with an uneasy glance at Catherine.

"Why, he was caught distributing these pamphlets that are stirring up feeling among the common people. The Ministers must find out from whence they originate. Much of the trouble can be laid to the Irish, I have no doubt, but it is the French who are the true, the vilest enemy."

"Are there any Frenchmen about?" asked Henry, surprised. "They should be easy enough to detect."

"Oh yes, to be sure, French sedition and treachery surround us as we speak," the General confirmed, with a gleam in his eye.

"We see no sedition in our part of the country, sir," commented Charles. "You will think we live a very quiet life, out of the world, in Hampshire, but I assure you we naturalists are most urgently busy in the summer months, so many observations as we have to make. But there is need for haste. The life-cycle of the beetle is desperately short."

"There are a great many dangerous characters in Gloucestershire," said the General, his frown deepening. "Men of the William Godwin sort, who preach anarchy, do nothing but help the enemy. Measures must be taken, or the country will be completely destroyed, I assure you. I fear you are not sufficiently alive to the danger all around you, Charles."

"Those whose concerns center upon ornithology have more important things to think about," returned Charles mildly, "and I can answer for there being no seditionists near us."

"Ah, that you know of, my boy. That you know of," said the General. "But inflammatory ideas are in the air, and there is no telling where it all may end, I assure you. You will take quite a different view of things after hearing our Member talk. Perhaps you will come to the hanging with me, and see for yourself."

Charles made no answer, and the General was distracted by looking at his watch.

"Good heaven! Here is calamity! Five o'clock, and dinner not even announced yet. You see how things fall into laxness when you are not at Northanger, Eleanor."

At that moment the butler entered, to make the announcement.

"Sterling! What do you mean by this delay? We ought to have been at table five minutes ago. It is a positive insult to the Viscount and Viscountess."

"It is no matter, Father," Eleanor hastened to say, as he took her arm with indignant ceremony and propelled her into the dining room, the others following in their train.

Catherine supposed that this meal would be very much a specimen of their visit. General Tilney dictated what every one should eat and should think, was conciliatory to the Viscount and Viscountess, distantly annoyed with Henry, and paid no attention whatever to Catherine.

The contrast with how she had been treated on her first visit to Northanger Abbey, when he had positively courted her, with so many small attentions as to make her uneasy, and his current treatment, was striking enough. Yet strange to say, she concluded that on the whole, his neglect was to be preferred to his attentions.

The abundance of dishes, the formality of the arrangements, the length of time the General deemed it necessary to sit at table, were all oppressive to Catherine, and she longed to be back at Woodston, alone with Henry. Whenever their glances met, she was comforted by knowing he felt the same.

A large remove of fruit was placed, with grapes, pears and peaches in the abundance customary at Northanger; and upon the silver centerpiece were two of the General's prize pine-apples.

"The pines thrive well, Sir, I see," said Henry, as he knew he must.

"Well enough. I can't say more. Wantage will never water them as frequently as I believe to be right; he must needs know best, and then there will be the devil to pay. It is an outrage, that he commands a salary of – I can hardly name it to you, for you will not believe it; but not a guinea less than two hundred a year is what this fine gentleman of a gardener demands."

"These plates are pretty, sir," Catherine spoke up, lifting a fruit plate, with the familiar little curling letters around its leaves. "This pattern resembles that of the beautiful tea-service you were so very kind as to send us, and for which I have to thank you."

"A small enough gift for my second son," he said negligently. "Neat, but pretty; unpretending. I am glad you can appreciate them."

"Indeed we do, sir, but I have been curious about the pattern. As with this service, it has what look like very small letters, twined round the outside of the leaves. Is there a message intended, we wondered?"

He waved a hand airily. "Just a little conceit of mine. A Latin benediction – it is a family tradition to engrave such things on our china."

"A benediction?" asked Henry, incredulously. "On the contrary, I thought, sir, that I could make out the word Malediction, or something very like it."

"You mistake, my boy. The engraver was desired to print the words of the blessing that is on our house. If he has done otherwise, we must write to him, to put the matter right. Let me know what you find, on further examination, and I will see to it."

In the ensuing silence, the General blandly offered Charles a slice of pine-apple. He inspected it closely.

"A bromeliad," he observed, "of Brazilian origin. In England, these cannot thrive outside a hot-house, and are consequently very expensive to cultivate."

"True, too true. There's no profit. Even at a guinea a-piece, we only sold an hundred last year. But it is always my prime pleasure to be the soul of generosity to my friends. I never think of myself, when I can do something to please the eyes and palates of my guests. I am perfectly indifferent to luxurious food myself, I assure you."

The General stopped and cocked his ear at the sound of an approaching horse. "By God, I wonder if that is not Frederick, come early," he exclaimed. "It would be like him."

Eleanor and Henry exchanged an apprehensive look, and Catherine had only time to hope that she would be able to greet Captain Tilney properly, despite her very great antipathy to him.

He entered, his tall military figure set off by his red coat and fine lace facings, and sweeping off his black hat, he made his bow in form. This gallantry had no effect on Catherine, who could not help remembering him unpleasantly from her visit to Bath. There he had flirted with her friend Isabella, even though he knew her to be engaged to Catherine's own brother. James had a lucky escape from Isabella, for she was as unprincipled as Captain Tilney himself, and had played him off, only to be deserted by Tilney, in her turn.

Such was the foundation of Catherine's dislike, and it had been in no way mended by his negligent and disrespectful manners. But the General beamed broadly.

"Frederick! Welcome, my dearest boy. Sit down and take some port to warm you. You have a great deal to hear."

"And I will listen, for I have damned little to tell," the soldier said languidly, throwing his long figure down in a chair and smoothing his silky mustache. "Been in town – we've got our orders. We're to be based in Northampton for the winter. There's for you, Sir. You can count on my spending more than half my time in Gloucestershire – can ride over at a moment's notice."

"Ah, that is famous," agreed his father, adding eagerly, "And did you hear much seditious talk in London? Pamphleteers, reports of rioting? What is the word?"

"Nothing of that sort, that I heard," he replied. "Only some talk of the Irish unrest, but that's old news now."

"You know who's coming here? Dunning, our Member, is bringing a party from London. You may conceive of the seriousness of the situation."

"Another political meeting, is it, sir?"

"Nothing to deserve such a name. But it would be irresponsible, in my position, not to be concerned. All the trouble can be traced back to the deplorable French influence. I am positive a network of spies is in place. They are certainly stirring up the laborers."

"But we have ladies here," drawled Frederick, peeling an orange, "you can't want to talk about politics before them. Ladies have no interest in such matters."

"Why, I have always had a great concern for politics, you know very well, Frederick," protested Eleanor.

"And I am trying to learn about the subject, too," Catherine made bold enough to say. "Is it your belief, then, that the French are infiltrating the countryside, to try to stir up a revolution in this country?"

The General looked momentarily angered by her having the temerity to speak, while the Captain wore a blank expression.

"There will be enough talk of that when our guests come," the General said shortly. "and is not for ladies. In the meantime, Frederick, I have a matter of a very different sort to take up with you. It is private, but we are all family here."

"Of what sort, sir?" asked Frederick, not without apprehension.

"Why, your marriage, my boy. Now that your brother and sister are married, Frederick, it is highly desirable that you, as the eldest, should quit the Army and settle. I have been considering the question, as you seem in no haste to do it for yourself. Your new brother, Viscount Eastham – Charles – has a most eligible young sister."

Charles looked surprised. "My sister Anne? But she is not sixteen," he said. "We do not believe in early parturition, in my family. A forced fruiting is unnatural, and unhealthy for any species. Consider these pine-apples."

"My pine-apples are not unnatural, by God, and their health is perfection," said the General indignantly. Then he subsided. "A pretty girl, now, with a fine fortune, is a very different thing from pine-apples. We can wait till the girl is a year older, or riper, if you prefer, my dear Charles. I am sure that Miss Anne will find Frederick very pleasing."

Charles looked quite ready to object, but Frederick forestalled him. "I am not thinking of matrimony at present, sir," he said decidedly, "and perhaps never shall. You well know that marriage is a positively dangerous concern, for men of our family."

It flashed through Catherine that he meant the family curse, and she glanced quickly at the faces of Henry and Eleanor for confirmation. Both appeared dismayed by Frederick's speech.

"My dear young fellow," said his father cheerily, "you don't suppose I believe such a myth? How then should we all be here, safe as houses, if there was really a curse on Northanger Abbey."

"The curse on the Abbey!" exclaimed Catherine, in spite of herself. "You don't believe in that, Captain Tilney?"

"On the family, rather than the Abbey, Miss Morland – Mrs. Tilney I mean," Frederick answered, grimly.

"And you are convinced it is true?" she persisted, incredulously.

"It's not to be talked about," he said, turning away abruptly.

"It is time for the ladies to retire," said the General, consulting his large and ornate French watch. "Frederick, I have not half informed you about the alarming state of affairs in the county that our visitors will be canvassing."

Eleanor assented, allowing that she was tired, and invited Catherine to go upstairs with her.

As soon as they were alone, mounting the grand staircase, arm in arm, she breathlessly began to barrage Eleanor with questions.

"Henry told me the story about the curse, Eleanor. But does Frederick really take it seriously? Do you?"

"No, my dear Catherine, I think it unfounded nonsense; though a belief in it has done this family a great deal of harm. Frederick only mentioned it to deflect the subject of marriage, I am sure."

"He spoke as if he believed in it. I was quite shocked."

"You might think that Frederick could no more believe in superstitions than we do ourselves; but I am afraid that, at times, he *is* half persuaded the story is true. This may be the effect of our mother's sudden death, and the blank it left in our lives. A man who believes in nothing, you know, can believe in any thing."

Catherine looked down. She was still ashamed of having once imagined that General Tilney had murdered his wife, but she had another supposition that she must voice.

"Eleanor, what do you know about the writing on the china?" she asked impulsively. "Is it really a family tradition to have blessings on the dishes, as your father says?"

"I know nothing about it," answered Eleanor hesitatingly. "My mother brought her china from her old home, and it was unmarked, in a willow ware pattern. My father has bought many sets since; he has a mania for – he likes china; but I never saw any with letterings before. He must have ordered those fruit plates very lately. You know, Catherine, that my father has his oddities."

Catherine stood on the stairs, thinking, her arm still linked through Eleanor's.

"What I wonder is, why does the General urge Frederick to marry, if the curse is supposed to fall upon his wife? And if he refuses, who is the curse supposed to fall upon then?"

"You must remember, there is no curse," Eleanor reminded her gently. "Let us not talk about curses and untimely deaths, dear Catherine. We should never be able to sleep! Come into my room, and we can read for awhile, before the gentlemen come upstairs."

Catherine was distracted at once.

"Oh, yes. I have the Lyrical Ballads in my room, that Henry gave me. Have you seen it yet?"

Eleanor smiled. "Poetry! That is a change. You used to love nothing but horrid stories," she teased.

"I hope I have a better taste now," Catherine assured her, placing her hand on her door. "Why, what is this?"

For a small sharp steely knife had been driven deep into the door. From it depended a piece of writing paper.

As Catherine took a sharp breath and turned pale, Eleanor stepped forward and took her elbow.

"My dear Catherine, what is it?"

"Please – take my candle - "

Eleanor held it and Catherine pulled the paper free. With shaking hands she read the terrible words written there:

"Bride of Northanger, beware the Maledict, that falleth upon you. Depart the Abbey in fear and haste, and nevermore return."

Chapter Five

"That's torn it," said Henry grimly, crumpling the piece of paper. "We leave in the morning."

Catherine and Eleanor sat on the bed, their arms around each other, and Charles stood in the doorway.

"What is to be done?" implored Eleanor.

"Have you questioned the maid?" Charles asked practically.

Young Annette was summoned, and stood there before the gentlemen and ladies, trembling.

"No, sir, I never seen that paper. It was not there when I went to get my lady's night things ready."

"Did you see any one else enter the room?"

"No, sir. Only – "

"What?"

"There's so many servants here," she said lamely.

"It is true, any one could have affixed that note to the door," Henry concluded. "My father did not do it himself, however; he was downstairs all the evening."

"Some one playing a trick, no doubt," said Charles gravely.

"But who would do such a thing?" asked Eleanor, distressed. "It cannot be one of our servants."

"Well, we won't get to the bottom of this tonight," said Henry, "and we will be gone from here tomorrow."

"I am afraid your father will be very angry if we go," said Catherine, distressed.

Every one was silent for a moment. It was too true.

"You cannot wish to remain, after such treatment," said Henry incredulously.

"I think we ought," said Catherine slowly. "We can all keep our eyes open, and question more of the servants. Some one is trying to frighten me away from Northanger, and I will not be easy, till we know who it is."

"Well, if you feel like that, Catherine," said Henry reluctantly. "I certainly shall not leave your side for a moment; and we will be gone in a few days' time, in any case."

Nothing more was said of the matter at breakfast; the General carried on with the subject of Frederick's marriage, and as if to stave off any more mentions of his sister, Charles kept up, with at least equal perseverence, a rival discussion of the bird species of Gloucestershire.

Changing tactics, the General began to urge Frederick on the advisability of an early visit to Eleanor and Charles.

"Of course, we should miss you here, and I do want you to meet our Parliamentarian, Dunning," he said, "but I should not stand in the way of matrimonial matters; and it would be an excellent time for you to meet Miss Anne."

Frederick looked mutinous, but said nothing.

"We will be very happy to have Captain Tilney visit us, perhaps later in the year," said Charles civilly, "but it will never do in early summer; I really believe, sir, that his only interest in birds is in the shooting and eating of them. In the winter they will be safe enough from him. Now, Eleanor, are our things packed? We must start out straight away."

Eleanor, in hastily directing the servants, only had a moment to whisper to the concerned Catherine, that they should return at a moment's notice if she summoned them in any distress.

They were soon away from Northanger, leaving Catherine to preside as the only lady at the tea table. General Tilney took no further notice of her, and he continued to openly berate his elder son.

"I am disappointed in you, Frederick," he said, with grave, reproachful looks. "A fine fortune – perfectly unexceptionable – you could have all that, and probably a girl of very pleasing looks and temper into the bargain. What makes you so stubborn, sir?"

"It is my nature, which I have inherited from you," returned Frederick angrily. "I will not be browbeaten into marriage, and you know very well why. The first son in this family has every thing to fear from the married state; and I by no means intend to subject myself, or any one else, to the like horrors that you, sir, and your father, and his father's fathers before him, endured."

"You are a fool, Frederick, to believe tales told by servants and nitwits! Of what are you thinking? You know very well that your mother was not struck down in early youth by some mysterious absurd witchcraft. She had a long standing internal complaint, and was past her fortieth birthday when she succumbed."

"I am not taking any chances," he replied stubbornly.

"Then what do you propose to do? Remain a bachelor all your days, and allow Northanger to descend to Henry and the string of brats that always seems to come to a rectory?"

"Oh!" Catherine could not help exclaiming.

"Sir, you forget my wife is present," Henry reproved him in a strong voice of displeasure.

"I do not forget it. At least you have a wife, however poor a creature, which is more than Frederick has. But she will hardly do, in respect to birth and fortune, to be mistress of Northanger."

"I am sure she does not wish it, nor will she stay to be insulted, much less threatened in notes and china," said Henry hotly, standing up as if to leave.

"Notes? What do you mean? Your impertinence, sir – "

But the General was interrupted here by Frederick striking the table, so that the complete set of breakfast dishes, which happened to be blue Jasper ware, rattled. "I tell you once for all, sir, I have no intention of marrying, and let this be an end of the subject between us, for ever."

"I don't fathom you. You have never met this girl; why be so solicitous for her? If she did die, you would have all her portion – a fine thirty thousand. Is that not good enough for you?"

"I have said my last word. I don't marry her."

"Then, pray, what will you do? For I can cut you off with a shilling, never forget that, sir."

"I have plenty of money of my own, from my mother's estate," said Frederick heatedly, "and never fear my being without female companionship. I can have as much of that sort of company as I choose. And it is not in your power to keep Northanger from coming to me. It is in the articles, and must one day be mine."

"Then why do you not care for its future state enough to marry and provide an heir?" thundered his father. "After all I have done, slaving for years to improve the place, and make it something worth passing on – and for whose sake? Yours. Yet you are ungrateful for all I have done."

"You have pleased nobody but yourself, sir, with your epicurean luxuries and comforts, and have always had things exactly as you like them. I mean to do no less, myself. My choice is to remain single."

Father and son glared at each other. Henry seemed to think of saying something, but thought better of it, and remained silent. The moment was only broken by the entrance of the butler, to announce that a crate of Venetian glass, long awaited, had just been delivered.

"Ah!" exclaimed the General, with animation. "I have been waiting for this, for many months. The choicest Renaissance glassware – rare design – exquisitely blown, uniquely twisted. Quite a history, too, once belonged to the de Medicis."

Frederick looked disgusted, and was heard to murmur, "More geegaws."

"They sound very magnificent," put in Henry, trying to make peace.

"Yes. Rich cobalt blue glass with flecked swirls of pure gold. And one goblet," he said, sinking his voice, "is peculiar in its qualities."

"In what way?" Catherine could not help asking curiously.

"It was made expressly for Caterina de Medici – another Catherine," he said, with a meaning look at her. "It is said that if poison is poured into this vessel, it will shatter - thus providing a warning to the one about to imbibe," finished the General with satisfaction.

"Are you expecting to be poisoned?" asked Henry, startled.

"I hope not; but only think of the cleverness of the conceit! There, my boy, you will never understand, you have no taste for the beautiful and precious, and Frederick has even less." He glanced at Frederick, whose face was stony, and then turned toward the distressed Catherine.

"You, young lady, I conceive, do have an eye for a pretty set of glassware. You may like to watch the box being opened," he offered, quite amiably.

Catherine assented politely, and she found herself, obediently if not very willingly, following him to his offices in the modern wing, where he forgot her presence in directing the servants to be careful while they pried open the crate so he might remove each glittering goblet from its paper nest.

Nothing untoward occurred, and Catherine began to feel somewhat reassured, supposing it possible that the General had not had any thing to do with the note.

The following day brought the party of gentleman to Northanger Abbey. Catherine was relieved to find her duties as hostess so slight as to consist of little more than her pouring tea, and she was made completely comfortable by Henry remaining by her side. Together, they observed the visitors with some interest, but without saying much.

Mr. Dunning, the Member of Parliament, was a short man with a loud voice who seemed to love the sound of it, while Lord Grey, an older gentleman, had a noble politician's polished geniality. With them was a man who was understood to be a French emigrant, or at any rate, to openly admit to having had a French mother. A man of between thirty and forty, Monsieur Blaine was introduced as a guest of Admiral Symonds, who had made his acquaintance in London. The others looked on him as a curiosity, and were disappointed to see that his dress was unexceptionable, that of an ordinary gentleman. The only oddity was a pointed beard and moustaches, very unlike the close-shaven faces and short *en brosse* hair of the rest of the male portion of the party. He spoke in a soft voice with a hint of French suavity in his accent, his manner contrasting amusingly with the expostulations and near-curses of the bluff, red-faced old Admiral.

Toward evening, another party from London arrived, and now the house seemed full of gentlemen. Following a long and elaborate dinner of ten courses, the visitors removed to the drawing-room for port and conversation. They debated with skill, though the only concrete point under deliberation was the continual danger posed by the warlike Great Nation across the Channel, and the machinations of Napoleon. The speakers employed a certain amount of cautious deference on M. Blaine's account; but the Frenchman himself was all smooth diplomacy, and assured the party that, in his opinion, the conquest and destruction of England was the very farthest thing from any French person's mind.

"Seditious ideas," M. Blaine was saying, in his softly accented voice, "have never come from France. It is your peasantry that is doing all the mischief – stirring up revolt, quite spontaneously."

"If you will permit me to contradict you, Monsieur, that is hardly possible," objected Lord Grey politely, "so stolid and loyal, as our country people are. Proper Saxons. They would never get such ideas into their heads, were they not put there."

"And by whom, that is the question," nodded General Tilney.

"There are too many revolutionists in the countryside, continental weasels," agreed the Admiral. "All this talk of burning down factories – and helping the Irish – and love without marriage – I tell you, the country is going to the devil."

"That is just what I say," M. Blaine agreed smoothly, and turned to Catherine.

"It is a pleasure to meet a jeune fille so charmante, of such surpassing air and beauty," he addressed her with a gallant bow.

"I?" asked Catherine, confused. "I am much obliged, Sir, but I am no young lady, or jeune fille as you say: I am a married woman."

"Ah, yes, but you see in my country, it is the married woman who has la liberte, the freedom. The young lady is closely guarded; the married woman is able, indeed almost expected, to form romantic friendships with gentlemen of the world."

"Not here in England," she said emphatically.

"Madame, you break my heart! And you with the form like Venus. You are wasted in the country, you should be in society, where you would be besieged by lovers, and I the first one of all."

"I should not like that at all," she said abruptly, and moved away.

"What do you think of the Frenchman now?" Henry whispered to Catherine. "I heard what he said to you, and should like to whip him."

"He would probably consider that a pleasure," she said bitterly.

"Catherine!" Henry was amused. "I had not thought I had given you any French novels to read. Come, let us sit over here, I think we will be safe. The gentlemen are more interested in the wine than the coffee."

He led her to the other side of the room, and they seated themselves by the coffee urn, away from the others.

"Oh! I have never been spoken to in such a way. How can he be tolerated in this company?"

"As you are the only woman, you are the one he has been making love to," Henry shrugged. "He is better with the gentlemen. But I do not like him at all. Quite apart from his manners to you – which I cannot dismiss - he breathes insincerity, and I suspect he has a hidden purpose."

"I wonder what it can be."

"Some double dealing, I have no doubt. He is certainly disingenuous in playing down the threat from the Continent. I can't think how my father tolerates him in the house. He hates nothing like a Frenchmen."

"Perhaps he will find a knife in his door," suggested Catherine, with some asperity.

Henry looked at her with concern. "Catherine – you have borne everything so nobly. Considering what has happened, I really think we will be justified in leaving tomorrow. With so many guests here, my father will take little heed of our departure."

"I would have no objection," she replied, from her heart.

Just then voices rose and Henry and Catherine looked over to see the Frenchman and General Tilney in argument.

"No, I cannot approve of your pamphlets, General. To me your hatred of the French is manifest in your writings and publications, as if you are accusing my nation of all evil."

"Why, what would you expect, after such wars as we have been fighting for all these years? You French are at the bottom of every thing, you cannot deny, wishing to undermine and destroy England by fomenting revolutionary ideas here. It is my duty to say so and to disseminate the truth in my pamphlets, to warn our government of the still continuing dangers!"

"Yes, it is men like you who have working to bring about the downfall of our Emperor, and the defeat of the greatest and most civilized nation in the world," expostulated the Frenchman with some heat. "I hold you to blame, General Tilney, both generally and personally. You have caused and are continuing to cause, unspeakable damage to my nation."

"Well, I'll be damned," exclaimed the General. "You say this in my own house? How dare you? It is treason, nothing short of treason, and you ought to be shot for it!"

"Let there be no further discussion," said Lord Grey, stepping forth with diplomatic authority. "We need not fight the wars here in Gloucestershire, and we must remember that Monsieur Blaine is our guest, deserving of our civility at least."

"Monsieur Blaine is not wrong," interposed Mr. Dunning, who relished an argument. "There can be little doubt that our excellent political pamphleteers have done a great deal to demoralize the French cause, and certain it is that General Tilney is one of the most adept and persuasive of their number."

"Yes, yes, fine writer, our friend Tilney," chimed in Admiral Symonds, "But knowing the French gentleman in question better than any one else here, I assure you that, foreigner though he is, Monsieur Blaine means no harm to England and the English in his own person. Do I not speak truth, sir?"

"Oh, to be sure," muttered the Frenchman, subsiding, though with a murderous glitter in his eyes as he still regarded General Tilney. "If I have offended any of this party, I proffer my apologies."

"Accepted," returned the General, with a contemptuous bow, "for the moment. After all, why should we hold resentment – we who will soon whip the French as soundly as whipping has ever been administered."

"You spout unfounded English braggadocio like a cur," Monsieur Blaine began fuming, but Admiral Symonds restrained him.

"Be sensible, man. We don't want trouble. We most of us understand how you feel, to be sure we do," he said in a loud whisper, "but it is better to say nothing."

"Quite," said the General coldly. "Now, I take it, our gathering is concluded for the night; you are welcome to remain and enjoy your port and cheeses – there is a very fine *yellow* Gloucestershire, the colour of a Frenchman's courage – or you my prefer to retire to your rooms; the servants have shown you where they are, and candles are on the table by the door. I have business to accomplish before I rest, and will say good night."

Catherine watched him narrowly as he left the room in some haste. "I wonder where he is going," she asked Henry. "It must be some awfully important mission."

"I try to stay out of my father's business," he said shortly, then softened to smile at her. "Shall we put him out of mind, and go upstairs?"

"Oh, yes. Henry, dear, will you go first and take the candles – I want to sit a moment, by myself, and think."

"Very well, Catherine, but if you don't appear pretty directly I shall come down again; I misdoubt that Frenchman's designs upon you!"

"I will be safe," she assured him with a smile.

After he was gone upstairs, she slipped out of the room and, making sure no one's eyes were upon her, made her way silently down the hall and stepped boldly out on the lawn. Some distance away she saw General Tilney's fine upright form walking hastily to the greenhouse, which was lit up inside by an ornate silver candelabra.

"What can he be doing?" she wondered, and moved closer. After a few moments she saw him exit the greenhouse with something like a bulky package in his arms and walk towards the oldest section of the convent walls.

"He is up to some secret and nefarious deed, I know," she said to herself. "But perhaps I can find out what he was doing in the greenhouse."

In a few steps she was at the glass building, and stepped inside. Wantage, the elderly gardener, was within, and looked up in some surprise from a table of food that he was rapidly covering up. She glimpsed what looked like trays of potatoes and cooked vegetables, odd things to find in a greenhouse.

"Why, Wantage!" she exclaimed. "What are you doing here at this hour of night? What is all that food for? What did the General want?"

As he covered the last tray firmly she was surprised to see his aghast, frightened expression.

"Oh, Ma'am!" he cried. "You didn't ought to be in here. It's as much as my place is worth. Please, excuse my bluntness, but do go, I beg, before General Tilney comes back. If he sees you it's all up with me."

"I am so sorry. Of course I'll go – only what is it all about? What are you doing? What is the food for? Is he taking it somewhere?"

"I can't tell you, miss, I'm ever so sorry. Only you could be in some danger, so please, by all that is holy, go back to the house!"

"Very well," she answered, perplexed, and obediently turned to go.

As she crossed the dark lawn to return to the house, she saw the General, now with no package, but holding only a candle, leave the convent building and walk rapidly back toward his own quarters. Frightened lest he see her, she quickly hid in the shadows and watched him go.

Looking back toward the convent, she was truly startled, frightened more than ever before, by seeing a ray of light from the moon picking out and illuminating a wispy, ghostly lady in grey. The figure, which looked like a phantasm, glided a little way in the direction of the greenhouse, and when Wantage put out his candles and left the structure, Catherine dimly saw the Grey Lady glide back to the dark building.

Never had she run in such terror before, as she sped back to the house, ran up the broad staircase, and darted into her bedroom.

Henry was surprised. "Catherine! Are you all right? Has something frightened you? Was it one of the guests – the Frenchman?"

"No, no," she cried, almost breathless. "It was nothing alive, nothing human! It was a ghost, Henry, I am almost sure. It was a wraith – a Grey Lady!"

Henry gave a tremendous start. "What! But Catherine, how could you know of the house legend, that Northanger is sometimes haunted by a Grey Lady at night? I don't believe I have ever mentioned it to you. Of course it is perfectly preposterous, but how singular that the thing you saw – if you did see something – should be that."

"I did see it, Henry," she said emphatically. "Do you doubt me?"

"No. I am sure you saw something. But it could not have been a ghost. It was someone playing a prank – we may not know who or what, but rest easy in knowing it could not have been any thing otherworldly."

"I think your father met with it too," she confessed, "I saw him walk into the convent wall, carrying what looked like food, and then the Grey Lady glided out after him to watch his return."

Henry looked disturbed. "I do not know what devilment my father is up to, any more than you," he told her, "but I must confess that for all his talk about his liberality and the improvements he makes to the estate, he has often indulged in shocking cruelty toward his tenants. It may be that the lady you saw was a tenant, and he has some arrangement with her something forced."

"Oh, how terrible, Henry! Can we not help her?"

"I don't know how we could. The estate manager, Claiborne, knows most about my father's business, and it is to be hoped, would prevent him from doing anything positively – criminal." He looked as if he hoped it was so, rather than believed it.

"We are safe enough here tonight," Henry went on, "and it is best to leave my father to his own peculiar devices. I dare not think what he is doing; and you ought not, either. Come, let us go to bed, and be together. Tomorrow we will be gone from this unfortunate place, and I will write to the agent when we are back at Woodston, to be on the alert for any shameful abuses. Not that he can prevent them, but my father will not like to have his excesses exposed."

Catherine shuddered. "I cannot wait to be at home, Henry," she said fervently. Undressing quickly she was soon in the warm bed, pressed closely against her husband for comfort.

Chapter Six

Catherine was picking delphiniums in her garden at Woodston, scarcely a week after their return, when a man on horseback was seen riding rapidly down the lane to the vicarage. Henry descried him too, from the window, and came out of doors to meet him. As the man dismounted, Henry recognized one of the Northanger servants, known to him from boyhood.

"Edward! What brings you here? Nothing wrong at the Abbey, I hope?"

"Yes, sir," said the servant breathlessly, wiping his face. "There is though. My master, I'm sorry to tell you, is dying."

"Dying! My father dying! Why, man alive, what has happened? Tell me."

"I will, sir. Though none of us is rightly sure what brought it about. He and them gentlemen – Lord Grey, and the Admiral, and the Frenchman, for the Londoners departed yesterday – they had a grand dinner, with all the best gold plate, you know, sir, and I was called on to serve. Well, after the savory (it was a nice cheese rarebit, brought on in the interval just before the fruit pies), they had the wine poured in them blue glasses that came last week, you recollect."

"The Venetian glass goblets. Yes."

"And all of a sudden, the one the General was holding, it broke into an hundred pieces!"

Henry had been listening calmly, but now he exclaimed in astonishment, "What do you say?"

"Yes, it broke, and that was not all, for he threw it from him, into the fire, and cried out that he'd been poisoned!"

Henry stared, unable to speak, and the servant continued his story with relish. "And then he fell face down, that he did, sir, with a terrible crash, his head in the fireplace, with a great gash on the crown. We summoned Dr. Lyford by express, and he said that to all appearances, the General must have suffered a stroke."

"My father is not dead, then?" Henry regained his voice.

"No, sir, not yet he isn't. He has moved and spoke once, and what he said was to ask for you to be fetched, in haste. Will you come, sir?"

Henry looked at Catherine, who stood quietly, trying to control her tremblings at the frightful news.

"Yes, certainly I will. Do you feel able to accompany me, my dear, or would you prefer to stay at home, and wait to hear of news?"

"Oh," cried Catherine, "I don't want to wait alone, without you. Please let me come. And your father will need nursing."

"You will not be called upon for that, I think; but there is no question that your company will be of the greatest comfort to me. Yes, Edward, Mrs. Tilney and I will ride back with you."

"There's one more thing, sir. There was that talk about poison – "

"Yes?" said Henry impatiently.

"And some are saying as how that there Frenchman, the Monsieur they call Blaine, done it."

"What do you mean, man? How could such a thing be possible? It is hardly within reason."

"Maybe so, sir, but the facts speak different. And that is, the Frenchman disappeared in the very hour it happened, last night – and he has not been seen this morning. Clean vanished and gone, he is!"

Chapter Seven

Catherine felt herself guilty in almost enjoying the twenty mile journey to Northanger Abbey in Henry's curricle. To sit beside him, watching his capable driving, and his handsome profile, while knowing him for her husband, was still novelty, and felicity itself. At first they made some desultory conjectures about the situation of his father, but with such scant actual information, and no real affection for the General on either side, the subject soon lapsed, and they fell into a happier mode of observing the sights of the countryside round, which gave rise to some delightful ideas for improving their own gardens.

Northanger was duly reached, however, and the curricle and horses were led away to the stables, while the young couple were welcomed by the distracted and white-faced butler.

"How is my father, Sterling?" asked Henry at once.

"Oh sir! He is very bad. There's no denying. The doctor is with him, will you join him now? You had better make haste, as it isn't at all certain he will be able to talk to you."

Without further discussion Henry and Catherine followed the butler to the General's handsome and high-ceilinged bedroom, where he lay under his rich embroidered canopies and blue silk coverlets as if already in state. The stertorous sound of his breathing could be heard along the corridor, when they were still at some distance, and they halted at the door, at their first glimpse of the struggling and sunken face upon the pillows.

"What is this?" Henry asked the doctor, sinking onto a divan and making room for Catherine beside him. "Has he had a stroke, then?"

"He may have done," Dr. Lyford answered, "and that is the intelligence I have given out to the servants, for the moment, but the most dangerous and peculiar part of his condition is something else. It is his throat."

"His throat?"

"Yes. You see, it is almost eaten away."

Catherine drew her breath in quickly and wavered, as if she felt faint. Henry poured water into a goblet from the bedside table and handed it to her.

"Is this too terrible for you, my Catherine?" he asked anxiously. "Would you prefer to retire?"

Before she could answer, a rasping whisper came unexpectedly from the bed. "No! She stays," croaked the General.

"He has not spoken before," said Dr. Lyford, leaning forward intently. "I did not believe he could. His life is ebbing – this state cannot last long."

"But what is it, Doctor? His throat, you say – is it a quinsy?"

"No, it seems raw and torn, from the inside, as if – as if he had ingested some kind of caustic substance."

"Caustic! Do you mean, a poison?"

"It may have been a poison. Only broken shards are left of the goblet from which he drank; it shattered instantly, by all accounts, and by the time I asked to examine some of the pieces, there was only a faint odor of the wine remaining. It could have been anything – a few drops of Prussic acid, or oil of vitriol; perhaps a compound to kill rats and birds."

"Oh, how shocking!" said Catherine. "Who could have done such a thing? Can he not be helped?"

The doctor looked at her gravely. "Any person in the house might have dropped something into the General's goblet, I imagine," he said. "No, there is nothing to be done for him. He is growing weaker and breathing more hardly."

"Can we call in any one else for consultation? A surgeon?"

"It would be useless. All that can be done is to nurse him, to administer to his bodily needs as gently as possible. We can give him nothing for the pain, for he cannot swallow; his entire trachea is burnt and a liquid in the throat would cause nothing but agony. He will die of thirst if nothing else."

"I – I do not like to leave him to the servants for nursing," faltered Catherine.

"It is a pity Eleanor is not here," Henry told the doctor earnestly. "She and her husband have gone on a visit to Lord Lymington, and are too far off to be easily summoned. And where is Frederick?"

"He has been out searching the neighborhood all day. I hope he will return soon," said the doctor. He looked at Catherine appraisingly. "You are very young, and it will not be a pretty job, nursing the General. But he does seem to wish your presence."

"I can't understand it," said Henry, "he generally attends to Catherine very little."

"If you are feeling equal to it, it might be helpful, it certainly would be a charity, if you would sit with him," advised the doctor.

"And I will stay with you, Catherine, do not fear," Henry told her. "This is a deathbed, after all."

"It will be easier for us to be here together," she answered faintly.

Hour after hour passed, with little change. The General seemed largely unconscious, though he moaned indistinctly, and he showed no sign of awareness when Catherine watered his brow or smoothed his coverings. As she and Henry watched silently, Catherine had sufficient time to consider how very strange it was that she should be nursing the man who was her former nemesis and virtually a bogeyman.

Rain set in during the night, and no sound was heard but its patter, and the General's struggling groans. Toward dawn, however, he became a little more restless, and seemed to be trying to sit up. Henry sat on the bed and supported him on his pillows, as his heavy eyes opened and fixed on Catherine.

"Oh thou, my daughter, mark what I say," he gasped out, "This is murder!"

"Don't try to talk, Father," urged Henry, as Catherine tried to conceal her horror.

"I must. Hear me, hear me now. The ghost, the ghost must be fed!"

And with that, the General fell back on his pillows, dead.

Chapter Eight

Frederick returned to Northanger a scant few hours after his father's death, and found his brother and sister-in-law in the General's study, where the doctor was writing to summon the coroner from the county seat.

"So, the old man is dead," said Frederick without preamble, flinging himself into a chair and stretching out his long legs. "Murdered, from the look of it. Well, he had enemies enough for that. Almost any one at that last house party could have done it, or most of the tenants, I daresay. They all hated him."

"You are jumping rather too rapidly to that assumption, Frederick," said Henry.

"And jumping is what you have to do in these circumstances. I made tracks at once, I can tell you, and have been everywhere about the place, but to no purpose. That Frenchman is certainly the most likely culprit, but there is no earthly sign of him, and no one knows where he may have gone."

"Have you been out all night, in the rain?" Catherine asked, concerned.

"No; put up at a cottage. Set out as soon as I'd spoken to the servants, as I would brook no delay in going after him."

"And you found nothing. Were all the guests at the dinner questioned?" asked Henry.

"Oh yes, every one, but not a soul had any idea of what had happened, or saw any one meddle with the wine."

"And now all who were there are long scattered, I suppose," said Henry, "most of them gone back to London."

"To be sure. Dunning has gone, but Lord Grey is staying with Admiral Symonds, and his seat is not far distant, you know, only ten miles or so. They may be able to tell us something more about the Frenchman, as it was the Admiral who introduced him at Northanger. Perhaps he and Grey may have some further information. Yes, I think you had better write to Grey, Henry. He is the more sensible of the two."

"I have summoned the Coroner," put in the doctor, "perhaps he will form a better notion of what has happened. The law requires that he be on the site within eight and forty hours."

"What about you, Frederick? Will you wish to question the servants again, more minutely?"

"Not I, no," answered his brother coolly. "The coroner is the man for that. What I mean to do is to set out again with the dogs, and some shooters this time, and hunt the Frenchman down, for once and all. We must find a trail somehow, though the rain is devilishly unlucky."

"He has been gone for some time now," said Henry doubtfully. "Would it not be better for you to remain? Our father is not even buried yet."

Frederick was curt. "He is however dead, and I am now the master of Northanger, Henry. And I shall do as I think best. My object is to find Blaine, by any means possible, and to exact no less than revenge."

"I hope you will do nothing rash," advised the doctor.

"You may count on me for prudence, sir. Now, Henry, I will collect the dogs and men and be off, as quickly as may be. I want to make the most of the daylight. Do you remain here and take care of the place. You can see to the coroner and all that sort of thing."

"Do you think it is seemly and respectful, Frederick, to be riding all about the country when our father – "

"Save your preaching for your pulpit," snapped Frederick. "I am going, and you may be grateful that I am good enough to show my trust in you by leaving you in charge."

"Very well, but I beg you to recollect that I must leave Northanger Abbey and be at Woodston for Sunday, to do my duty to my parish."

"Don't fret, little brother. I assure you I shall track down the culprit well before your return."

Frederick and his men rode away with a clatter of hoofs and yelping of the dog pack, leaving Henry and

Catherine to handle the unfolding concerns of the disarrayed household.

Friday brought the coroner, Mr. Carter, and an assemblage of jury men to Northanger Abbey, where the inquisition was to be held. Admiral Symonds arrived too, to join other witnesses, guests and servants, there gathered. Henry watched the proceedings with interest, though Catherine's presence was not required. After the business had been adjourned for the day, it was then time for Catherine, as lady of the house, to preside over the pouring of tea and serving of a collation for the visitors.

"Have they reached a verdict?" she asked her husband privately, when they had a moment alone in their room before going downstairs.

"Not yet," Henry replied, "but I suspect that the coroner will decide that it was a natural death, possibly brought on by apoplexy."

"Apoplexy! But how can that be? What about his throat – the damage? How can it have been due to anything but that?"

"Dr. Lyford testified that there was apoplexy, and he could find no concrete evidence that any poison was used, for none was found. The stroke may perhaps have been occasioned by the shock of the goblet shattering in his face. And the throat damage might be put down to disease, after all."

"Do you think that is a fair assessment?" asked Catherine incredulously.

Henry lifted his shoulders. "You must understand that it would be an embarrassment for the coroner, don't you see, to give a verdict of murder when there is no sign of a murderer; it would not look well."

"Look well! How on earth could that matter? And to whom?"

"All sorts of people," he said dryly. "Come, let us go down now and see how it is. If we both keep our ears open, it will be well."

In the drawing room they were approached by Admiral Symonds, who addressed Henry in his loud voice, as if he was shouting orders aboard ship. "My boy," he bellowed, "I am glad to see you and your good lady. And to find a moment to tell you that your father was one of my very old friends. He will be a loss to us all, and to the entire county, I may assure you."

"Thank you for saying so, Admiral."

"No matter, no matter. I am only sorry there was nothing more I could say, in evidence."

"I am wondering about that. You were present, Admiral. Did you see nothing at all that looked like – well, like a poisoning?"

"As I said at the inquest, assuredly not, my boy. The glass broke; your father fell heavily, no doubt owing to the crash and perhaps to a touch of apoplexy. Yes, that seems like a reasonable conclusion to me. What a very great loss it is, to be sure. His books – his conservatory – his pine-apples. What will become of every thing?"

"The estate now comes to Frederick," said Henry evenly, "and he will decide how he will dispose of his property."

"You do not believe that he will resign his commission, and take up residence at Northanger? He will be much needed here."

"Frederick is his own law, and I cannot presume to speak for him, sir."

"Of course, of course. Well, time will tell. Where is he, then? It makes a very odd appearance, his being absent, at such a time."

"I am afraid he has gone off again, with some hot headed scheme of revenge," said Henry with a sigh. "I don't know how well you know my brother – he has an impetuous nature."

"Chasing a slippery Frenchman, already long gone without a trace! Upon my word, it is a bad business. He may as well try to catch a will-of-the-wisp as that slippery creature."

"Slippery? Did you think he was that, sir? Yet I understood that he was a friend of yours."

"Not to say a friend, just one of a thousand acquaintances such as every naval man has," replied the Admiral hastily. "Met him in London, at the Royal Society, where scientific questions are discussed, always of interest to military men, you know. It was a meeting of navigators, and he was introduced by one of my fellows, Admiral Carlisle, whom he had been questioning about naval routes. An interest in shipping he had, being from a merchant family he claimed; but now I am rather doubting his veracity. Hindsight is a famous thing."

"And how did you chance to bring him here?"

"A fortnight ago he wrote that he was passing through Northampton with a view to settling nearby, and had a strong inclination to see me again, and meet some of the people who would be his neighbors. He mentioned General Tilney particularly – repeatedly in fact. I did not decline to make the introduction, though it did occur to me that his interest in my friendship with the General was passing strange. Well, well, at any rate, that was how I came to bring him here, at his own request."

"It does sound as if there was some deliberate calculation at work there," Henry considered.

"Does it not?" said the Admiral with animation. "I now wonder, what with his being so unforthcoming about himself, and taking such a speedy departure, if General Tilney's instincts may not have been right after all, and spying and sedition was at the bottom of every thing. If it proves to be so, I shall always be chagrined at having been taken in."

"It might not be the case at all," Henry reassured him. "It must all be conjecture, for now. I hope Frederick can find him, but his actions are so rapid and unconsidered, I frankly doubt his success."

"I am sure as shooting that we will never hear of Blaine again, and the Coroner will issue a verdict of natural death. I heartily hope so, as any other outcome is hardly respectable. I should hate such a thing to happen in my own county. Murder and sedition have no place here. And now I had better take my departure; I am most sorry about your father. Shameful, shameful."

Chapter Nine

Henry left for Woodston as late as he dared on Saturday night, not liking to leave Catherine, but knowing he must preach the sermon at his church in the morning. The coroner and the doctor were still in residence at Northanger, occupied in details of post-mortem, so Henry felt she would be safe enough with their protection, though an atmosphere of such morbidness was hardly what he would choose for his young wife. Still, it would only be for two nights, and there was every probability that Elinor and Charles might return before he did.

"Never mind, Henry," his wife told him briskly. "I am no longer a fanciful girl, given to fears. I hope I am able to do without my husband for such a trifling amount of time, until your return on Monday. It will pass quickly, I know. You need not worry about me."

"I am relieved that you can feel so, Catherine. Woodston is only a few hours' distant, and I will preach as quickly as I possibly can." He gave her a reassuring smile. "You will dine with Mr. Carter and

Dr. Lyford, pleasant gentlemen they are, and tomorrow you should have a peaceful day enough. Perhaps you may read in the garden, if it does not rain."

"Yes, Henry," she said. "I will try something of Maria Edgeworth, though I would much rather you read it to me."

"*A Practical Education?*" he asked with an arch smile. "That will provide some useful knowledge for when we are so fortunate as to become parents. The education of little children is a subject to distract you from the gloomy present."

"Yes, Miss Edgeworth does not write exciting novels, but something cheerful and instructive might be called for at this moment. However, I was thinking more of reading *Patronage*. That is why I wanted you to be the reader, for you have not read it yet yourself."

"No, but if you like it, I can catch up with you on my return. Three fine large volumes, and a very good story, I understand. Yes, you will be well occupied."

"I am glad of your approval, I would not be easy without it," she said teasingly.

"You are not really my pupil, Catherine, but my wife," he said with a sweet smile. "Being your senior, and consequently several years better read, my recommendation of books may be of some use; but I would not dictate. I have seen only too much of that in my own home."

"So I should suppose," agreed Catherine. "Your poor mother."

"And Eleanor," he reminded her. "So I would only advise that it might be wise not to return to your girlhood fondness for horrid tales just at this time. Mrs. Radcliffe would not be the most reassuring companion for a sojourn at Northanger Abbey, under these circumstances."

"Certainly not," said Catherine decidedly. "I mean to be strong minded, and not to encourage myself in foolish terrors."

He laughed, and gave her a most tender kiss, before taking his departure.

The doctor and the coroner were considerate gentlemen, and although they had not much to say over the dinner of roast pork and apple-sauce, they did refrain from referring to the proceedings they were engaged upon at Northanger, which could hardly constitute very palatable dinner-table conversation. Only after the meal concluded, and Catherine joined them in the drawing-room, did the coroner revert to the subject.

"Mrs. Tilney, I dislike to mention these things, but feel you ought to be informed that Dr. Lyford and I have concluded our examinations of the General. There is no more to be done, yet unfortunately, he must needs remain here, until the court officially concludes its business on Monday."

"Here? You mean – in his chamber?"

"Yes; we have prepared him for burial, and the coffin is neatly closed and covered. There is nothing to see that will disturb or frighten you. It is to be hoped that both his sons will return with dispatch, so the funeral may be held."

"My husband will certainly be here on Monday, but I cannot speak for Captain Tilney."

"But can the Court's verdict be given without the presence of the General's son and heir?" the doctor asked the coroner, perplexed.

He gave a slight shrug. "It may have to be so," he said.

"Should the funeral be held off until he is present?" Catherine inquired. "It would be a shocking thing if the eldest son were not here for his own father's funeral."

"You must know something more of his habits than we do," said the doctor. "Have you no surmise as to the length of his absence?"

"No, indeed. Who can say how long it will take him to find that Frenchman?"

"If he ever does."

"There's one more consideration," advanced Mr. Carter. "I hesitate to point it out, but it is necessary that some member of the family be present to spend the night watching over the unburied body. Of course a gentleman would be preferred, in the usual case; but unfortunately, Mrs. Tilney, you are the only family member here at the moment."

"Do you mean – you cannot wish me to sit up with him?" she gasped.

"It is customary. The family usually mounts a vigil so as to prevent any tampering with the body."

Catherine was aghast. "But – what could I do?"

"There is a divan in the room. I think you would be comfortable enough. The coffin, as I say, is well concealed, and battened down, and there's nothing to alarm. You might lock the door, should that give you a feeling of more security, with your husband away. And the servants, not to mention the doctor and I, will be nearby, should you want any thing."

Catherine was silent. Even in her most lurid girlhood fancies, and hair-raising perusals of horrid novels, she had never heard of a heroine, or any young woman, having to sit up all night locked in with a corpse; and certainly in her wildest imaginings she had never imagined that she would have to do such a thing herself.

Chapter Ten

The little servant Annette ushered Catherine into the room, and stood still a moment, timidly. "Is there any thing else you might be wanting, ma'am?"

"No, I think not, Annette," she answered, trying to sound matter-of-fact. "You have my dressing things?"

"Yes, ma'am, your wrapper, and linens are on the divan, and the toilet things on the table. We have removed - *his* - things."

"But *he* has not been removed," said Catherine with the ghost of a smile.

"Mercy, ma'am, no!" said the maid, moving backward in horror. "Oh dear me, I don't know how you can stay in here - with that there corpus. Oh! I'm sure I'd rather die."

"Don't say so," said Catherine reassuringly, "there's nothing at all to be afraid of, you know."

Together the girls looked toward the enormous canopied bed. In the flickering firelight, they could only discern the family banner, scarlet and gilt, laid heavily over the rise in the middle of the bed.

"That heavy banner covers every thing, you see," said Catherine in a tolerably calm tone.

"Oh, ma'am, I was afraid there would be, well you know..."

"What, Annette?"

"Oh, the smell – the smell of mortification, to be sure! I'm sure I'm sorry to mention such a thing." She bobbed a courtesy. "But thank goodness there is not."

Catherine shuddered. "What an idea! But no, indeed. Every thing has been well sealed up, I believe, and we are in no danger of any such unpleasantness."

"If you don't mind my asking, ma'am – why is it that they make you, a lady, sit up all night with – that?"

"Why, I am unlucky enough to be the only family member at hand tonight," Catherine told her, with a sigh. "I never thought of such a thing, and I know my husband did not. However, Lord and Lady Eastham are expected at any moment, and so it is only for this one night."

"But tomorrow is Sunday. Will they do Sunday-traveling?"

Catherine paused a moment, uncertain. "I hope – I believe they will think it justifiable, under the circumstances."

"But why must you be shut up here?" the maid persisted.

"Mercy! It is not being shut up, Annette. I am not a prisoner."

"I don't see the sense in it, ma'am, if you will excuse my saying so."

"It is thought necessary to guard a, a deceased person before burial," Catherine explained. "It is a tradition, lest there be any depredations from an intruder. If any thing happened to prevent a proper Christian burial, you see," she paused impressively, "it would endanger the deceased's immortal soul!"

"You don't say! Oh dear me! That would be bad, wouldn't it? But then, what if enemies broke in and tried to steal the corpus? Or a, a limb of Satan to steal his soul! Sure, you must be all a-tremble!"

"What frightful ideas, Annette! But no; who would come? Northanger is safe as houses, with so many menservants, and good Dr. Lyford just a few rooms away. No, Annette, I shall not allow to let silly fears prey upon me, and you must promise me the same."

"Well, you are very brave to be sure, ma'am, and if you do want any thing, there is the bell," she indicated the pull, "and I'll come myself, that I will, even if it is the middle of the night and to the room of a dead man!"

"You are very kind, Annette, but you may rest easy. I am sure I shan't require you."

"Don't you want me to help you undress, and brush your hair? I do that for Miss Eleanor when she is at Northanger - Lady Eastham, I mean, as is now."

"No, I think not. I will just sit here awhile, and then perhaps lie down on that divan."

"Oh! Excuse my saying, but I should go right to sleep, if I was you, ma'am, as quick as ever you can. It is the best way to get this night over with!"

"Yes, that is good advice. Good night, Annette."

The little maid departed, but Catherine had never felt less like sleeping. Yet strangely she was not afraid. She remembered that other night at Northanger, a night of fears that she never cared to think about, not because the terrors were so frightful, but that they should never have been at all, and were only due to her own foolishness. It was her own folly and weakness, and her shame at exposing them to Henry, that she hated to think of. Yet that night had, she hoped, cured her of such imaginings and fears, and had made her a more sensible and serious woman for ever after.

So it was with tolerable coolness that she, confident in her newfound maturity, now surveyed the General's bedroom. It was the very opposite of anything Gothic, or ancient; it was like nothing out of *Udolpho*, or *Otranto*, or *Vathek*. General Tilney had a passion for both modernity and luxury, and his own room had been fitted up as handsomely and comfortably as any man's in the kingdom. The divan, chairs, couches, were solidly well upholstered, in pretty fabrics of pale rose and dark Burgundy French stripes. The large, heavy mahogany desk was not tooled over with fanciful carvings, but instead had a heavy but simple slab of marble on top, and was fitted out with every appurtenance to be found in the best stationer's shops.

It was at this desk the General had pored over his pamphlets late at night; there was his lamp, in the shape of an onyx blackamoor, and there his piled correspondence, and the very pamphlets themselves. Catherine remembered him once telling her how he attended to important matters late into the night while she rested her eyes for mischief; but she had felt little curiosity about the pamphlets, sure that they would be dull and stupid.

Now she wondered if she should think differently now, after her course of reading with Henry, and its consequent maturity of mind. Rising, she went to stand by the desk and glanced at two or three of the papers. They were much as might be expected - "seditious unrest in the Home Counties" - "organization of the Gloucestershire militia" – "the uses made of a network of spies" - "preparations for penetration against a surprise enemy." The letters too - she recognized the great names of some of his correspondents at the top of the pile. The Home Secretary, the High Sheriff of Gloucestershire. Nothing of much interest there, not even to a grown up, married, better educated Catherine.

Curiosity she still had, however, about the family she had married into, especially now that she knew that it did have a secret history, and a mysterious curse. The family legends did not alarm her – much, but she felt she would like to know more about them, whatever they were. Henry and Eleanor had made light of them, yet there was the way Henry, the night before their wedding, admitted that however spurious were the tales, it was an undoubted fact that the oldest son's wife in every generation, had actually met with a terrible fate. This sounded straight out of a horrid novel, and despite being cured of reading such works, how curious, how ironic it was that she should find herself in a situation that almost seemed like living in one.

Catherine hastily reminded herself, for the dozenth time, that she need have no fears, in trying to find out the meaning of the family curse, for she was not the wife of an eldest son. But there, she was forgetting there was no reason for fear, for curses and legends were imaginary, the stuff of superstition. It must be only a chain of coincidental circumstances after all that had killed all the first wives of the family. Any one who read history knew that the most dreadful things, murders and burnings, accidents and torture, had happened with appalling frequency back in the olden days; and the more ancient, the worse they were. It was the events of an uncivilized, ignorant past age, that were reflected and stirred up for sensation in the kind of fiction known as horrid. Any modern, rational, educated person knew that.

Turning from the desk, Catherine wondered where the General would have kept papers dealing with his ancient family history, for certainly such papers there were, and they must be somewhere. The desk was plainly for his daily concerns; family papers must be safely stored somewhere else.

There was a heavy ornate chest in the alcove under a window, with some curios and glassware on top; exactly the sort of chest where old papers might be kept safe and dry. She had a reflexive dislike for old chests now, ever since the mortifying moment on her first visit to Northanger, when a promisingly forbidding manuscript concealed in such a chest proved to be nothing but a gentleman's laundry list. Still, she would not let any former foolishness stop her from the type of sensible explorations that she intended to make now.

It was the work of only a few moments to remove the glassware and figurines, which were rather ugly, she thought – one was a nasty little metal satyr, another a grinning monkey's face carved in old wood. For a man of taste, she did not know why the General would keep such things, but perhaps they were family heirlooms.

The chest was locked, with a large old-fashioned clasp, but Catherine had seen a key-ring inside the desk, and when she retrieved it she instantly noticed a key that looked just the sort of age and shape to fit into the lock of the chest. And fit it did. Delighted with her own perseverance and deductive powers, Catherine had no trouble in opening the lock, and then lifting the top of the chest, which took some strength. Holding her breath, she looked within.

She saw, lying on the floor of the chest, an old inlaid marquetry box that looked as if it might contain jewelry, or something precious; and equally exciting, beside it was a thick and ancient pile of manuscript writings. She wavered a moment at which to investigate first, but she had trafficked so often in old manuscripts in her late reading, that she did not hesitate. The manuscript pile was unwieldy, the size of an old Bible, full of papers that crumbled in the most delicious ancient way, and she lifted it out with some little difficulty and carried it to the desk. Setting her lamp there, she seated herself in the General's capacious chair, and began to read.

To her surprise, it was a fairly fresh and new paper, in the General's own hand, that lay on top of the rest.

> "To my heirs and assigns,"

she read, but immediately saw that despite this language, it was not a will or legal document, but a letter.

> "I am commanded by the force of my heritage to write this account, which may be perused by all my blood descendants; but is of most particular interest to the eldest, my son Frederick, who will in all probability be the first to read this after my death."

Catherine paused, and reflected if, by the rules of honour, she was entitled to read farther? Henry certainly was, as his father's blood, but she was not a blood relation. Still, he had mentioned "assigns," and she was surely Henry's assign, if it meant, as she believed, being heir or successor to an interest in his property. She was of Henry's own body and flesh now, bound by ties of marriage, she reasoned; and in short, she would continue reading.

> "The details of my life ought by rights to be well known to my descendants. Born and bred in Gloucestershire, at the home of my ancestors, the venerable Northanger Abbey, I was the oldest son, and heir to a fortune as fine as few private men in the kingdom can claim. In spite of my wealth, however, I always had an abhorrence of being idle, and my father was well able to keep up his property and interests on his own until late in life, without my assistance; so he agreed to what I wished, that is, to enter into an active career. Accordingly, I entered the military, and with his interest and my own abilities, my rise was rapid; you will know how I served with distinction under General Cornwallis in America, rising to Commissary General of his forces.
>
> Subsequently, on the death of my father, I returned home to assume the mastership of Northanger Abbey. For many years I also continued my military work in my own county, making myself useful in helping in the organizing of the militia forces and supplying their troops. Since my retirement, I have tried to run my own estate upon military lines, as in these days expenses are tremendous and an establishment such as Northanger must perforce pay for itself. A gentleman of leisure cannot sit down and

expect every thing to prosper around him, unassisted. I trust my descendents will profit from my labour, the legacy I leave them; but there is another and more awful legacy that I cannot help but transmit to them, albeit most unwillingly.

My own mother predeceased my honored father by many years; and he, in accordance with family tradition, explained the matter carefully to me, as I remembered the event only dimly, it having occurred in my extreme youth. I only recollect my mother bleeding excessively, and had a glimpse of her lying pale and near to death, when I was taken to bid her farewell. My father told me that she exsanguinated from a copious nosebleed, that occurred when a stone from the ruinous part of the Abbey fell upon her head as she sat in her beloved garden. There was no stanching the fatal flow; and all who witnessed the accident were convinced that this was in fact nothing less than the operations of the family curse. My father's mother too was taken in a similarly swift manner, though in her case it was a sudden seizure of spasms that attended her shortly after his birth.

Naturally skeptical, and not given to fantastical tales, I nevertheless grew up to be convinced of the curse upon my family, and fearing its consequences. My own father's narratives, and that of his father's, and their progenitors for ten generations before, have all been carefully preserved in this selfsame box, and are here for the next generations to read, and try to come to terms with as best they can. If any way can be found to break this terrible inheritance, you have my prayers and wishes that the reader will be the one to do it, though I confess to some doubt that inventive investigation is the particular forte of my son Frederick. Henry might have greater success, with his clever mind; but he and his are not in the line of fire, so to speak.

Frederick, you will recollect that I once tried to give you a hint of our condition, some years ago when you were just commencing your military career; and you will also remember how often I have vainly urged you to make a practical, prudent marriage, one that would bring money and security into the family, without involving your heart over much. If your wife must suffer a terrible fate, it would be better to have a financial arrangement rather than a marriage of sentiment that would only involve your own distress.

With the fortunes of Northanger secure, as they now are, it may be possible that persons of science and reason be employed in studying the ways to break the curse on our house. I entreat you, Frederick, to follow every possible avenue of inquiry. At the same time I state yet again my strongest wish that you should marry, beget an heir, and get the curse over with as quickly as possible for this generation. So far you have resisted and disobeyed my wishes, showing a leaning not to marry, but to keep mistresses. Foolish boy! I have warned you of the consequences, and attempted to warn Henry too, by sending him a coded gift, as it is not permitted by tradition to speak out in warning to any but the first son; but to little effect. Now circumstances must be left to take their own courses, if I should not survive long to direct matters according to my own commands.

There only remains for me to say that I have suffered greatly from this curse on my family, which has affected my whole life profoundly, in the premature death of my own mother and the fate of my wife. My attempts to fortify the house and establish a sound financial footing for my heirs, have done nothing to keep the blows from falling. Nor will your abstention from marriage, Frederick, keep the curse away from you and yours; I am not permitted to know or say how this will happen, but the ancient manuscripts are only too clear about what will transpire if you do not marry.

If I myself have met a suspicious death, if you suspect me of having been murdered, be sure that it is almost certainly so; and I lay upon you the sacred duty of avenging your wronged and tormented father, lest worse happen to you all and your heirs until the end of time. Know that I go leaving your father's blessing upon you, and hope it will not prove to be yet another curse upon this house. Farewell."

Chapter Eleven

Catherine's teeth chattered in her head as she finished this terrible missive. Her blood ran cold, her heart was pounding, and as she went to the couch to snatch up her shawl, and bundle herself up in it, she thought hard about the document had read. The General really did believe in curses, it seemed; what was not certain was whether he was deluded, or even mad, though in life none had seemed more practical and business like than he, pragmatic to a fault. She did not know what to make of it, but after some contemplation she returned to the desk, thinking that there would be more to learn by leafing through some of the older manuscripts that lay beneath the General's letter.

There was the letter written by his father, telling of his wife's early death from the terrible nosebleed, and the seizure suffered by his own mother. The letter beneath that one, was that of the General's grandfather, who had been born in the seventeenth century, and whose curling, difficult hand was hard for Catherine to read. But she made out that his wife had indeed died by spasms, and his own mother of a sudden ague at the age of nineteen. My own age, thought Catherine with a chill.

There were letters of Tilneys written through the 1600s, and back into the 1500s; then there was a crumbling sheaf of documents which Catherine gathered referred to the suppression of the monasteries, the dispersal of the monks, the destruction of the Holy Blood, and more details of a very gory history.

There followed the account of how Northanger Abbey had come into the hands of an early Tilney, by the gift of King Henry the Eighth; since which date one son had always been named Henry. But she had read enough. A monk's curse! Her own husband named after a veritable Bluebeard of a king! It was all as fanciful and lurid as any romance of horror; yet it was perfectly real. An unknown monk had truly laid a deathly curse upon the family, and the eldest Tilney in every generation had believed in this, throughout the centuries. Even a Godless man, a self-styled rationalist and evident materialist, such as General Tilney, had been oppressed by this curse, and perhaps been driven half mad by it after all. Considering this history, Catherine felt revulsion, along with, reluctantly, some stirrings of pity.

And now there was Frederick, the new master of Northanger, to consider. The General had doated upon his eldest son, favored him over Henry and Eleanor. Perhaps, she conjectured, after the loss of his wife, any remaining capacity for affection had been burned away, and only Frederick ever stirred any remnant of fondness in him. He had been a poorly judging parent, who could see no fault in this son, dashing but unprincipled though he was. For the gentler and unsoldierly Henry, General Tilney showed little beyond an irritated contempt, and his only daughter he had turned into a servant. Perhaps the real curse which the General had imparted to Frederick, had been the system of treatment that resulted in making him what he was, and what the General had been himself: selfish and heartless.

Frederick, like many soldiers, Catherine knew, was superstitious, and had not liked to be reminded of the curse; that might be why he shied away skittishly from making a marriage predestined to tragedy: he determined to avoid the misery of the curse by the simple solution of never marrying at all. His logic must be that the curse would then fall upon Henry and Catherine, for he cared little about Henry, and about Catherine, nothing at all. But was that the terms of the curse? The General's words and the materials in the ancient documents seemed to indicate that no matter what Frederick's machinations, they would only end in his own destruction.

Disheartened, Catherine scarcely knew what to do. She disconsolately put the manuscript back where she had found it. Then she recollected the marquetry box that lay beside it. She had little curiosity left; who could want to find more secrets of this sort, of such a family? But almost listlessly she unfastened the box, and opened it to find a dark, leathery, hairy object. Attached to it with a hempen cord was a note in faded brown ink that read:

"Here lyeth the dried hedd of Lady Margaret Tilney, my beloved wyfe, killed by an arow while out a-hunting; and her little Catt, her dearest object in life."

Catherine flung the hideous object from her, and noticed with a shudder the small shrunken gray fossil relic that must have been the poor dead woman's pet cat. Stifling an inadvertent scream, she hastened to the door, and flung it open, but then stopped. How could she leave? If she summoned the servants, the doctor, the coroner, the men, every one would know she had been poking into the chest, reading documents perhaps not meant for her to read, and discovering terrible secrets that were not hers to share. She must put the horrid things back, at once. Oh, no heroine she had ever read about, had ever had to do any thing so awful!

Yet she must stay in the room this whole night – and she could see by the General's large clock that it was a quarter past four. Morning was almost come; she would not have to remain in this terrible place for much longer. Collecting herself, she took a piece of linen, and gingerly used it to pick up the horrid dried head, drop it back into the chest, and close and fasten the lock again.

With the first gleamings of crepuscular pink light starting to show in the long windows, she went to gaze out at the beautiful dawn scene, hoping to find some serenity. To her shock, she was immediately shaken to discern a face out in the garden, gazing back at her!

She almost shrieked, but clapped her hands over her mouth, and steadying herself, took another look.

It was a woman, none other than the same Grey Lady she had seen before. She was standing some twenty feet from the house, in the semi-darkness, and Catherine could not distinguish much about her, only that she was clothed in diaphanous grey, and was as pale as the moon, with skin that was white, but wrinkled. As she watched, the wraith lifted her arm to gesture, and mouthed a single word. What was it? It seemed to be "Oh!" or perhaps – "Go!"

Catherine could not tell, but she could look no more. She felt rather than saw the Grey Lady gliding away across the still-dark lawn, as she pulled the curtains closed.

As she did so, her hands felt something resting on the sill, a piece of cloth. She pulled it inside and saw that she was holding a small square piece of tapestry, or crewel-work, about eighteen inches square. The pattern, tightly stitched in delicate wools, was so intricate that it looked as if it might have taken years to work; and it was something like a sampler, with flowers and fruits on the outside edges, and a central pattern of an imposing house that looked very much - yes it did – like Northanger Abbey.

The sampler effect was owing to a series of words which, in motto-like fashion, circled the lozenge that enclosed the picture of the Abbey. The letters were tiny, interspersed with pairs of white birds that looked like doves, and at first Catherine was unpleasantly reminded of the small words in the message on General Tilney's gift of wedding china. Would this prove to be another malediction?

Nervously, she tried to read the message, but the size made it hard to decipher. She had to hold her candle between herself and the tapestry, and pore over it to make it out. At length she succeeded, and on reading the first words, she gave a great start:

"O new Bride of Northanger!"

it read.

She looked around apprehensively. That was certainly meant for no one but herself; there could be no doubt now that it was a message for her. Indeed, the Grey Lady must have left it. Shivering, she read on.

"Fear not, my dear daughter, for I lay only blessings upon you and your marriage. I wish you both an unbroken peaceful and fruitful life, this side of Heaven. As a mother who has suffered untold torments, I stand as the Guardian of Northanger Abbey against the wicked and the cruel, and hope that my love will enfold and protect you for ever, unto eternal life."

"Well!" exclaimed Catherine. "What can this mean? *Is* it from the Grey Lady? She must be real enough, however, for this is no work of imagination. Not only is it tangible, it is as sturdy and well-stitched a piece of needlework as I have ever seen, upon my word. Only, that poor lady's fingers! And her eyes! To embroider so many, many tiny letters! That, to me, would be the torture."

She read the precisely stitched message again carefully.

"No, I do not know, I cannot conceive what on earth to make of it. I will ask Henry, when he comes."

She set the tapestry aside carefully, and still breathing rather hard, and feeling more unsettled and shaken than ever, she thought some more about the message. She misdoubted her decision to show it to Henry, after all. It seemed to refer to his own lost mother, for whatever reason; perhaps the madwoman, this Grey Lady, had some fancy about Mrs. Tilney. Such a message would certainly be unspeakably painful for Henry to see, or to think about, and the more she considered, the more she positively dreaded to show it to him.

She could come to no conclusion, but even now Catherine did not even dream of attempting to undress or to try to sleep: that would be impossible. Wrapped in her shawl, she curled up on the divan to sit and to wait for the full dawn.

Chapter Twelve

Catherine had fallen into a light, chilly doze, when she was awakened by Eleanor and her husband, who came hurrying into the General's chamber, still in their traveling clothes, not long after sunrise.

"Oh, my dear Catherine, Sterling told us you had been made to sit with my father all night!" exclaimed Eleanor in a rush, as she embraced her sister-in-law.

Catherine was really thankful to see her. "You can't think how glad I am that you are back! But you must have traveled all night. How tired you must be!" she cried with relief.

"Yes, it was a long journey, but we had good lamps, and there was the three-quarter moon," Charles explained. "In any event, we are here now, and you need not remain in this room for another moment."

Eleanor looked around her father's chamber in distress. "The idea of leaving you in here, with the coffin! What an ordeal! Such a thing should never have been."

"Do not be alarmed, Eleanor, it does not signify. It was quiet all night, and I was not frightened. Not very," she amended. "I did fancy I saw something – strange – out on the lawn, toward dawn. But I will tell you all about it later."

"I don't see how any one could permit you to keep such a vigil. It was very wrong. Henry could not have known it. Why was it done?"

"No, Henry did not know it," Catherine answered, "but Mr. Carter, and the doctor, thought it was needful for a family member. It was not very pleasant, but I knew nothing could really happen to me, and you see nothing has."

"Well, now we are here, and I shall watch over the body, if any body must," Charles said firmly. "Until the time of the funeral. Do you know when that is likely to be?"

Catherine did not, but they heard footsteps and voices in the corridor, and Dr. Lyford and Mr. Carter appeared.

"Ah, good morning, you have arrived, Lady Eastham, and Your Lordship. Mrs. Tilney as you see has very nobly stepped into the breach and watched over your father in your absence, and we are very glad she should be relieved. You may like to retire to your own room now, madam."

"I certainly shall," said Catherine with relief. "I have not slept, and I wish to freshen myself and rest, after some breakfast."

"Yes, let us give orders for breakfast at once," agreed Eleanor. "And Mr. Carter – my husband is wanting to know when the funeral is to be held?"

"That is for you and your brothers to decide, my lady. We can proceed almost as soon as they have returned. The court will come to its formal conclusions tomorrow, on Monday, and the burial can take place as early as Tuesday."

"That gives us sufficient time to notify my father's friends and associates in the county," Eleanor considered, "and Henry will return Monday, will he not, Catherine?"

"That was his promise. Only we do not know where Frederick is."

While the party was at breakfast, and Catherine satisfying herself with a boiled egg and brown bread while the travelers helped themselves to a more solid repast of cold meats, a carriage rolled up to the Abbey and the sounds of the servants attending to the horses could be heard.

"That must be Frederick now," Catherine observed, "it is too soon for Henry."

It was so. In a few minutes Captain Tilney strode into the room, looking disheveled, as if he, too, had been traveling a long way, and had the help of some few bottles of wine. With him was a very young girl whom he held by the hand. She was cloaked, but a mischievous face, sparkling eyes, and tumbling copper curls could be discerned.

"Frederick!" cried Eleanor, jumping up. "Thank heaven you are here! We had no notion where you had gone."

"Now, Eleanor, there was no need for worry," he assured her. "Though I do have some news to tell. First let us eat – looks very good – our journey has worked up a hearty appetite. Sit here, Harriette, take off your cloak, and have some of these chops. We have been traveling long enough without sustenance."

"I will!" and the girl tossed off her cloak, revealing a gown cut very low, showing a tiny waist and more of her bosom than would be thought proper except at an evening ball.

"Will you introduce this young lady, Frederick," asked Eleanor politely, "and permit us to know how she comes to be here?"

"This is Harriette – Dubochet, I think you said you are calling yourself?" He turned to the girl. "And I'll tell you the whole story when we have ate. Harriette, this is my sister, Lady Eastham. Now pass those chops."

A servant sprang to pass the platter and for a few moments there was no sound but the newcomers' hungry eating, while the others looked at each other with expressions of some wonderment.

"There, that's better," Frederick said at last, pushing his chair back. "Shall we go into the drawing-room? For I have, as I said, things to tell."

"So we collect, Frederick," said Eleanor, and turning to the young lady, asked concernedly if she would like a shawl to cover herself.

"No thanks, I'm quite warm," the girl said carelessly, and Frederick took her by the hand to lead her out.

When they were all seated by a comfortable fire, the coroner was the first to speak. "But where have you been, Captain Tilney? It is urgent that we should be able to consult you upon all matter of business, now that you are the master of Northanger Abbey."

"All in good time," he replied. "I'm dreadfully tired; been rampaging all over the countryside, you know."

"And to no avail, I suppose," inquired the doctor. "There was no sign of the Frenchman?"

"On the contrary, there was," answered Frederick to their astonishment. "Found him in a tavern, in Cheltenham, if you will believe me."

"You found him!"

"Aye, I did find Monsieur Blaine, and I questioned him smartly, you may be sure. I was ready to take him into custody myself if I thought there was due cause."

"That you could not have done," interposed the girl, "for you were both far too drunk."

The others were taken aback, but Frederick only laughed. "You don't know Harriette," he told them. "The most outspoken girl of her age in all England. There's nothing she won't say, and quite the wit she is, too."

Nobody knew quite what to say to this, so the doctor pursued, "So you encountered Monsieur Blaine in a tavern?"

"That I did, and he was such a great talker, even oiled up with drinks as he was, that he convinced me he had nothing to do with my father's demise. Why, he swore that General Tilney was the finest man in England, and he would never have harmed a hair on his head, nor had he any reason to do so."

"And you believed him?" asked Mr. Carter disapprovingly. "I confess I am surprised you did not bring him back for questioning, at the least. That would have been the right mode of action to take."

"I daresay it would; but I was so tired by then, after riding two days with the dogs, and Blaine plied me well with wine, cunning devil, and then there was this young lady."

"But who is she?" asked the doctor as they all gazed at the girl, whose cheeks seemed, Catherine saw with surprise, to be painted.

"Harriette's the name, he told you already," she said pertly.

"She was with Blaine, don't you see, and he made her over to me, as a kind of distraction, I suppose it was, now I am in my senses."

"Great heaven! Frederick!" exclaimed Eleanor.

"Brother, this is not fit for ladies to hear," Charles objected.

"Well, if it is fit for Harriette to do it, it is fit enough for my sister and Catherine to hear, for they are fully grown married women, which she is not."

"She is very young," said Eleanor pityingly. "How old are you, my dear?"

"Past fifteen," said the girl pertly, "and I didn't mind coming along with Captain Tilney, for he told me he lived in a castle sort of a place, and I couldn't stand that dirty stinking Frenchman for one more hour."

"But how did you come to be with such a man?" asked Eleanor. "Did he – abduct you?"

"Oh, he picked her up in Cheltenham, where she was trying to hawk her wares, I suppose," said Frederick.

"You were selling something?" Catherine asked innocently.

"Only herself," Frederick sniggered, but stopped laughing in the face of their silence. "To be sure, 'tis no laughing matter. The girl isn't important; it's the Frenchman. Now that I've had time to consider, I could kick myself for letting him slip through my hands, but he scarpered when I was occupied with her."

"Ran away, do you mean?" asked Charles.

"That's it. But I recollect, now, that he did say something about him and my father disagreeing, for my father was always ranting against the Great Nation, you know. Blaine imagined he was a threat, having it in for all Frenchmen like that; and he was afraid that they could not both live in the same countryside. His wish was to settle here, but that would mean the General had to be dealt with. Oh, there was more; and now my head is clear, I consider Blaine must be some sort of a spy. He assured me that he would not stoop to murder, but I suspect that he is the murderer we seek, after all. Curse me for a fool, for letting him slip through my hands."

"What a misfortune," breathed Catherine.

"Yes. It is indeed," said the coroner, "I confess I looked for more sensible actions from an officer of your caliber, Tilney. Now what is to be done? Shall we send out the militia?"

"Oh, don't bother," put in Harriette confidently, "you have only to wait. I am sure the Monsieur will come back for me."

As it happened, Harriette was more nearly right than she knew. That night, all beneath the roof of Northanger slept deeply, and no one could discern the sounds made by the approach of a visitor. It was none other than the Frenchman, Monsieur Blaine himself, who stealthily entered the precincts of Northanger Abbey, as the parish bells chimed three. Tying up his horse at some little distance, he approached the house on silent footfall. His mission was at least in part the very same that the bold young Harriette had named to her incredulous listeners: he had come back for her. If he had the further motives of a spy, no one would ever know it.

With only the partial moon to light his way, yet determined to enter the house unheard and unseen, he slipped into a cellar entrance. This led into a subterraneous corridor, and the intruder felt his way by sense of touch, pacing slowly around twists narrow and winding. It was utter blackness, and the passage mazelike and intricate. Stopping, baffled, and aware that he knew not how to find his way out again, he considered that there no use pressing any further in this blackness. He must wait until morning let at least some small ray of light into the underground passages to show him the way. There was nothing else to be done, and no likelihood of any one finding him in this remote abandoned part of the Abbey. With philosophic resignation, he lay down, covered himself in his greatcoat, and slept.

Still in darkness, Blaine was awakened by a glimmering of light, and jumped up startled at the sight of a lady wearing long diaphanous grey robes, and holding a single flickering rush candle.

"Mon dieu! What are you?" he exclaimed.

She did not answer, but only gazed at him, with a quiet, mournful demeanor. "C'est une fantome," he gasped. "Can you be a ghost?" Stricken and startled by being wakened by such a spectre, he rapidly retreated backwards, but only to stumble, lose his balance, and smash unseeing into a gigantic outsize suit of iron armour that stood in that corner of the corridor.

The strength of the collision caused the iron structure to topple and there was no escape from the monstrous thing. The Frenchman scrambled to evade the falling armour, but there was nowhere to move in the narrow space, and the heavy contraption crashed onto the hapless man, hitting him full on the skull. He lay there, not moving.

The lady gave a small involuntary cry, but stifled it, and after a moment she gathered herself and knelt beside the man. Even by her dim light she could see that his injury was catastrophic, and could not but be imminently fatal. His skull seemed to be crushed and he was bleeding terribly. There was not a hope that she might be able to move the armour off him, or slide him from under the behemoth; there nothing for her to do at all but to watch helplessly as the man's breathing slowed.

In moments it was over. He was dead. The lady in grey knew not who he was, nor why he had come there. Was his death divine retribution for some unknown sin? Was it connected with the curse on the house, and had he interfered with its appointed path?

The poor lady had a muddled fog of curses and sins in her disordered mind, and was far beyond being able to puzzle out what had happened. She had been quite helpless in her own plight for so long, that she was unable to act; and even if she had wanted to do so, she could not, for she was by now faintingly weak. Crossing herself, she murmured a prayer, and retreated, silently tottering back into her chamber. Knowing very well that there was nowhere else she could go, she fell onto her bed, insensible.

Chapter Thirteen

The travelers and Catherine sought their rest, while the coroner and doctor wound up their business, writing to several officials scattered about the countryside, to spread the alert regarding the fugitive. On Monday Henry was at Northanger by noon.

Catherine had never been so glad to see him, and he was equally relieved, though concerned to hear of what she had endured. She did not tell all, holding back for the moment the story of the tapestry, but what he did hear was enough. Earnestly she assured him she was quite unaffected and unharmed, but he could see from her paleness, and her degree of relief at seeing him, that she had indeed suffered.

"I blame myself," he said, "I ought never to have left, at such a time."

"But you were obliged, Henry. It is your duty to be at Woodston for the church and parish affairs belonging to Sunday; that cannot be controverted."

"No; but I might have taken you with me. It was wrong to expose you to being on your own in this place, which I know has always made you nervous; and right at the time of my father's death. It was badly done."

"Oh, do not talk as if I was a fine lady with fancies and vapours, Henry. I might be trusted to take care of myself, for once."

"So you might." He caressed her fondly. "You do have great good sense, Catherine, and I must learn to rely on your powers of mind, more. I have been so used to trusting only my own judgment, and have thought it so superior that it has tended to make me think meanly of others."

"You have every right, Henry, because you are so very clever; and you are never mean."

"Not mean in the sense of being spiteful or cruel, perhaps; but you will have perceived by now my unfortunate habit of thinking lowly of other people's intelligence."

"You must have thought meanly of mine when we first met," said Catherine with a sigh, "I was such a silly girl."

"I have regarded your intelligence as rising more highly every day," said Henry with a smile, "and since your falling in love with me, have been convinced you have shown yourself to have the most excellent taste and judgment."

"You make me laugh, Henry, but I do not know what you will think of my judgment when I tell you all."

"I have perfect trust in your judgment, and you could not now persuade me otherwise," he declared.

"Well, then, I will tell you. I have seen the Grey Lady again."

"Catherine! Not really. Why, my dear girl, you must be quite mad after all!"

She exclaimed, and he had to point out that he was not being serious.

"But really now, you did see that woman again?"

"Yes, she was peering into your father's window at dawn, as I was watching there. She was trying to tell me something, but I do not know what, and she ran away."

"Good God, how positively chilling! And as if you did not have enough to unsettle yourself, that night. Really, I am amazed at your composure, for not falling into hysterics; I am sure most people would have done."

"No, I did not think she meant me any harm, in fact I know she did not, because she left me something, a sort of message in a piece of tapestry. I believe she meant to be kind. But I will tell you about that later. Just before, I had seen something so very much worse, that I - "

"I know, the coffin," he interrupted. "Well, and so we still do not know who your Grey Lady is. I did mean to have a word with Claiborne about it, for he knows all the people and tenants around here; and I will."

"I wish you would. But I have not yet made my confession to you."

"What can you possibly have to say now, my dear Catherine?"

"The thing I saw before the Grey Lady – it was not just the coffin."

"What in heaven's name was it then?"

"Oh, Henry, it is hard for me to tell you, but you of all people, are tolerably well acquainted with what my uncontrollable curiosity is. I had no right to do it, but spending that long night in that – that room, I dared to open a chest…"

"What, again?" said Henry, unable to keep from laughing a little, despite himself. "Another chest? I thought you were cured of all that sort of thing, and would never open another one as long as you lived."

"I am sure I never shall again," she said earnestly, and told him about the letters, and the relics.

He was struck by her account. "Well, I cannot criticize you – it was natural enough. I will only say that in this case, you may reflect that curiosity did not kill the cat, it found the cat."

"Oh, Henry, be serious. Remember we are in a house of mourning. You should not make me laugh."

"My dearest Catherine, as you rightly deduce, my meaning was to make you laugh, so as to lighten your feelings a little. You did nothing wrong, and I am sincerely sorry that my family should have such horrors in its secret coffers. So that is where the family history is kept. I will have to look those papers over myself, some time."

"I never want to see them again," she shuddered. "But you probably should look them over. They are a very complete family record, quite unique in the world, I should say. So much tragedy in one little box! It will make you quite sad."

"Look here, Catherine, we have vowed always to be honest with one another, have we not? Therefore I can say that it will not have escaped your notice that there is not much of sadness or sincere mourning going on at Northanger."

Catherine could not gainsay it, and would not tell a lie.

"That being the case, we will be fully justified leaving for home directly after the funeral."

"It can't be directly enough," said Catherine fervently. "What a house of horrors it is. I cannot compassionate you enough, for having had to grow up here."

"It was not all bad," he told her mildly. "There was my mother then, and dear Eleanor, and my brother was at times a good humoured companion. And there were all the country pleasures, and I was much absorbed in my education; no, no, Catherine, you need not be sorry for that."

"No, I suppose not. After all, it made you what you are, did it not? You could not have been so wise, and of such a good temper, without some shade in your life."

"You are right in principle; levity needs to be tempered with some compassion, or it is heartless."

"And you do have a heart," she told him with a caress.

"You are a philosopher, my Catherine, but I am going to take you to bed in spite of it."

Together they retired, both thankful that perhaps as early as the following night, they might sleep in peace in their dear own home.

Chapter Fourteen

Nothing more, naturally enough, was heard of the Frenchman at Northanger Abbey, though Frederick twitted Harriette about her certainty that he would return. Officials throughout the county would remain on the alert for a passing Frenchman who might be able to shed more light upon the General's sudden decease; but as the chance of his being found was now thought so slim, the coroner could see no reason why the case should not be closed. Accordingly he prepared to hand down the final verdict that the General had died of natural causes, and to give permission for the funeral to take place as soon as the family chose.

He had a final private word with the doctor before concluding. "I confess to not being entirely easy in my mind, Lyford," he said.

"No. I can see that. So often, in my business, cases of this sort have no clear determination. It occurs far more often than the public thinks, and we must take care not to enlighten them, lest we stir up alarm. It really cannot be helped."

"If I did not know the people involved, I should suspect it to be the fairly common phenomenon of a family member who murders a tyrannous older relation."

"Certainly I have seen such things, but you cannot think that possible here, can you, Carter?"

"Why not? Captain Tilney was present at the final dinner."

"I know, but in all the witness accounts, there was no slightest indication of him doing any thing untoward. There is no evidence."

"He had opportunity, just the same, and probably motive," the coroner argued. "He steps into one of the most considerable fortunes in the country. And then, there is the younger son."

"You can't think of Henry Tilney as a suspect?" the doctor said incredulously.

"With an irascible, overbearing man like General Tilney, the gentlest family members are known to reach a breaking point."

"Why, man, he was not even at Northanger, but at his parsonage, twenty miles away, the entire time."

"A short enough distance for him to have slipped home at night, and tampered with the goblet."

"Oh, come, come. Someone would have seen him, or his horse. And besides, he is a clergyman. His entire character speaks for himself."

"Some of the most principled people in the world have been driven to desperation by a tyrant."

"Well, if that is your thinking, why not suspect the naturalist? He might have possessed some poison to kill vermin or predators."

"He was hundreds of miles off. Now you are being absurd, Lyford."

"As is this whole discussion."

"Well, well, I only wanted to consult with you, and free my mind entirely. I am relieved to have your opinion, and I assure you I don't mean to pursue this line of thought. I shall sign the inquest verdict at once."

The service was accordingly held on the Tuesday at the Northanger parish church, with a goodly gathering of the General's rich and important friends and neighbors present, as he was buried amongst all his Tilney forbears in the churchyard.

The visiting mourners remained for the shortest time possible to politeness, after the General was duly committed to the earth. The burial over, they gathered at the Abbey for a rather speedily eaten collation of funeral meats before ordering their carriages and driving away in twos and threes, with no more haste than might be considered decently respectful to the family. Good county relations must be maintained, and no offense taken; but no one had really liked the General very well personally, and the occasional grudging presents and accompanying stream of braggadocio his neighbors had received from him over the years, left very little in the way of warm memories of the man in any one's mind or heart.

As soon as the last guest was gone, Henry determined on having an audience with his brother before his and Catherine's own departure. Frederick he was sure preferred to avoid any discussion, and accordingly Henry had to search hither and yon for him, until he found Captain Tilney in the General's own bedroom, sitting on the velvet-spreaded bed, his boots on a pillow, and young Harriette curled up by his side, *en negligee*, and entirely at her ease.

"Good heavens, Frederick, I have been looking for you every where," exclaimed Henry. "What are you doing in our father's room?"

"I beg you to observe, since you inquire, that it is my room now," Frederick answered in a tone that could only be called lordly. "This chamber belongs to whoever is master of Northanger, you cannot deny; and that is myself, which you will not deny either."

"No; certainly not. But our father's body has scarcely been removed for a matter of hours. Would not common respect, prevent you from taking over his chamber immediately, and putting your boots and your lady upon his cushions?"

"Do not be absurd, Henry. What's his is mine, and the General is now safely beneath the earth and can have no opinion about what I do with his plaguey fanciful cushions. As to what I do with my pretty girl," and he nuzzled Harriette openly, "why, my father always had an eye for a good looking woman himself. I remember when he was quite struck with your Catherine."

"Frederick, that is an observation that is really surpasses all boundaries of taste and decency, not to mention showing no respect for my wife," began Henry, angrily.

"I do protest that you are being a great bore," replied Frederick. "Remember that you have no authority over me."

"I never supposed I had," said Henry, even more incensed, "but I would remind you that while I may have none as a younger brother, as a minister, I do have a final duty before I leave, to remonstrate about your keeping a young woman at Northanger for purposes of immorality."

"It's me who might complain about that, if anyone has the right," put in Harriette saucily. "Tis none of your business, you are a sour puss for such a young man, upon my word."

"Frederick, can you not see that this girl is little more than a child? However she may have been thrust upon your notice, you must be aware that you are responsible for her welfare. Has she no home we can return her to?"

"I wouldn't go back there," cried Harriette, "for a hundred pounds! My father beat me and was as stingy as a rat; my mother was so worn out she was useless, after having birthed such a litter of girls, and my sisters were all horridly mean and jealous. I'll never go home, that's flat, when there are the jolliest good times to be had out in the great world."

"But, good times or no, you must know that it is not right to live with a man without matrimony, as you are doing," said Henry earnestly. "Surely your mother, despite her burthens in her own life, taught you that? We all must fear for our immortal souls, as we are told in church."

"It is against my religion to listen to any preaching," said Harriette. "It is a dead bore, and I always do the opposite of any thing long nosed old ministers say, I assure you. Not that you are old, and you would be quite a pretty man if you were not so pious."

"I hope you are not talking seriously now, Harriette, for your own sake. And as for you, Frederick, I know that you are perfectly aware it is a sin to take part in the corruption of a young girl."

"There; now you've had your say, and we've been pretty damned patient to listen to it," said Frederick shortly. "Suppose you take your leave now, brother. Harry and I have things we want to do in this bed, and we are not so dead to decency as to want to do them in your presence."

"I see there is no use talking to you," said Henry gravely. "Miss Dubochet, if you feel any access of conscience and wish to seek honorable protection, you may write to me at Woodston and I will come to fetch you at any time."

"You won't be hearing from me on any such account, I can promise you that," she assured him, tossing her head. "And when you do hear of me next, out in the great world, it won't be as Dubochet – I am resolved I won't be making my wretched family's name famous. I shall call myself something else from now on – Wilson. Never mind whose name it is."

He said nothing, but acknowledged her with a small bow and troubled expression.

"Well, be off then, brother," ordered Frederick. "When I am finished with my pleasures here, I have business to do. I mean to sack a whole regiment of servants today. My father's extravagances were absurd. That greenhouse! Damned pine-apples! That high priced gardener goes, instanter."

"You are the master of Northanger, Frederick," Henry only confirmed, and left quietly.

Chapter Fifteen

Henry and Catherine convened with Eleanor and Charles to discuss what was to be done. All agreed that there was no use remonstrating any further with Frederick; none of them could have any influence with him, and as he was determined to go his own way at Northanger Abbey, there was nothing any one could do.

"We all want to go home," Charles observed, "but Eleanor and I have been thinking of breaking our journey with a stay of a few days at Bath."

"Would you not like to join us?" urged Eleanor eagerly. "It is not in your way, 'tis true, but we have been thinking that, after all Catherine has undergone, a little time in Bath would be cheerful for her; and we should like to spend time together, and with you, in happier circumstances than we have yet done."

Henry looked at Catherine to see how she liked the suggestion, but he was not left to wonder long, for she clapped her hands in excitement. "Bath! I could see my dear Sarah! Oh! I do wonder how she is liking it there. And the Allens! They are with her, and how I should enjoy seeing them again! But where would we stay, Charles? In an hotel?"

"I keep a house in Bath," he informed her, "it is very convenient for observing the butterflies of Somerset, and I go to visit the Harestreaks and the Metalmarks every summer. Once I was lucky enough to glimpse a rare Duke of Burgundy."

"They sound quite like society families," Henry observed.

"Oh, how wonderful," exclaimed Catherine, unable to restrain herself from jumping up and down a little in her glee.

Henry smiled at his sister. "It is worth it to see Catherine looking so animated and happy for the first time in days," he said. "Let us go. I had already arranged for a friend from Cheltenham to take next Sunday's service at Woodston, on account of my father's death, so there will be no obstacle. Shall we take our two carriages?"

The plan was followed, and the travelers set out that afternoon. Catherine was always happy to be riding in their own carriage with Henry driving, and as they trotted away from Northanger Abbey there were more feelings of relief bordering upon elation among both young couples, than they could easily express, even to one another.

"I wish you could have got that poor girl away from Frederick, however," Catherine told her husband. "We might have brought her to Woodston, and sheltered and taught her, and perhaps in time found her a decent home and situation."

"We could not have kept her at the parsonage," objected Henry. "She is a Magdalen, you know, but more than that, I do suspect that she is the sort of character who simply causes chaos and destruction to every thing she touches. She could hardly stay under the same roof with a decent woman; and I don't know which of the two would find it more unendurable."

"Still, a cottage might be found, and she might be given instruction, and perhaps pay for her keep by doing some needlework and the like," Catherine persevered.

"I cannot imagine Miss Harriette in a cottage, can you?" said Henry raising an eyebrow.

Catherine reluctantly had to admit she could not.

"I should not like to be so uncharitable as to think that anyone is incapable of reform, but if ever there was such a girl, born to stir up trouble in the world, she is the one."

"How sad! Only think if it was our Sarah in such a plight."

Henry laughed. "No, that too is beyond my imagining. Sarah is no Harriette."

The distance they had to travel was closer to forty miles than thirty, and because of the late start they only reached as far as Stroud that evening, putting up at an inn; but they rode into Bath not much past noon on the following day.

As soon as they had been welcomed by the servants and disposed of their luggage at Charles' handsome house in Landsdown Crescent, Catherine, with the encouragement of the others, hurried away to the lodgings in Pulteney Street where the Allens were staying.

She was greeted rapturously by Sarah, and as warmly by the Allens, with whom she had always been a favorite. They were sitting with a young man Catherine did not know, but who was introduced to her as Mr. Speedwell, a lawyer, visiting Bath with his father who was taking the waters for his gout. He was a handsome young man with engaging, unaffected manners, and it was immediately evident to Catherine, seeing Sarah's sparkling eyes and pretty smiles, that she was decidedly smitten with him.

Sarah was wonderfully improved herself, and in her few weeks in Bath had blossomed to a remarkable degree. A good-looking girl of seventeen, with hair lighter than Catherine's, she appeared to advantage in the new fashionable clothes, ordered with the greatest of attention and care by the dress-conscious Mrs. Allen, and which gave her the look and air of a distinguished young lady of the *ton*. Looking at Mr. Speedwell looking at her, Catherine thought that Sarah's liking for him was, as nearly as she could tell, returned in kind.

"Oh Catherine," asked Sarah, "will you and Mr. Tilney come to the Upper Rooms with us tonight, and see the dancing?"

"I cannot tell," Catherine returned, "I should like it of all things, but you know we are here with Eleanor and her husband, and I must see what they plan. I daresay they will be quite agreeable."

"And I will be dancing," said Sarah in delight, "with Mr. Speedwell. He has asked me for the first two, and who knows what else we will do?"

"Have supper together, certainly, and it is to be hoped with you and your party, Mrs. Tilney," he bowed.

"And tomorrow, we think of walking in the Lower Rooms, by the river, after breakfast."

"Oh! I know Charles was hoping for a country walk," said Catherine, "perhaps you might come with us? He wants to see the Somerset butterflies."

"I should like to see the butterflies, would not you, Mr. Speedwell? Mrs. Allen, might I go see the butterflies? It will be with Catherine and Mr. Tilney."

"You may if you like," responded Mrs. Allen placidly, "but I hope you will not get grass stains on your gown, in a country walk. I beg you to wear your oldest one."

With suchlike plans in store, the days in Bath were certain to pass delightfully. All Catherine's party liked Mr. Speedwell, and he joined in most of their doings, to Sarah's high glee. Mrs. Tilney and Lady Eastham were confirmed as most acceptable chaperones, and the young people could do very much as they liked together, with blitheness the order of the day.

It was a damper on their happiness, however, when on the Friday night, entering the Upper Rooms where the grandest ball of the week was in progress, the young party were surprised to see none other than Captain Frederick Tilney, dancing with his Harriette.

"Why, Frederick, how came you here?" asked Henry, during a pause in the dancing.

"How? The same way you did, I perceive, in a carriage. Bath is free to all who wish to enjoy themselves, I think, always conditioning that they have the money. I might ask what brought you to this frivolous scene, when you ought to be rusticated in your country parsonage?"

"We accompanied Eleanor and Charles part of their way home," Henry replied without rancor, "as we hoped that the ladies might find Bath a contrast to what the gloomy scenes at Northanger have been."

"I can see how that would be," Frederick conceded. "Well, then, brother, I hope you all enjoy yourselves. As for me, I am going to dance." He turned, but his partner was gone.

"Why, where is Harriette – " he said, surprised. A moment later she could be discerned, dancing with a slender, aristocratic looking gentleman of thirty with powdered hair worn in the old fashion.

"Who is that she is dancing with?" he expostulated.

"That is Lord Craven," Mr. Speedwell, who knew every body, put in helpfully.

"Oh, is it? Well, I'll have something to say to him, for stealing my wench. Harriette, what do you think you are doing? You come right back here to me."

She made an impertinent little *moue* at him and did not stop dancing. "That's all the more reason I should not dance more than two dances with you. It is against the rules here, simpleton, and although not much of a stickler for such things, I had a whim to obey."

"The impudence! Harriette, stop dancing at once, I am taking you home."

"Excuse me," interposed Lord Craven, "the young lady is under my protection for these two dances, and I suggest you do not interfere, else I shall have to resort to the Master of Ceremonies."

"Oh, have her and be done with it then, I am sure I do not care a farthing," Frederick snapped. "And she costs considerably more than a farthing." He turned away in displeasure.

Mr. Speedwell looked grave. "Ought you to interfere?" he asked Henry. "Every body in the room must have witnessed that little scene. That young lady and your brother – I fear a full-blown scandal is brewing before our very eyes."

"I am very much afraid it is," Henry sighed. "It is what we look for, from Frederick, I am sorry to say."

Sarah looked anxiously at Mr. Speedwell, to see the effect of the incident on him, but he said no more.

The pleasure of the ball was punctured, and it was an anxious evening.

In the morning, however, the party gathered by appointment for a butterfly-watching party, and cares seemed to vanish with the golden sunlight. The warm grass and sprinkling of wildflowers of a fine hot English June forenoon were what was needed to blow away the ballroom's hothouse dramas.

In the fields and lanes, Charles was particularly in his element, for the summer life about them was in the most perfect state for study. He did not try to capture or kill the butterflies, but noted down what they were and where he saw them, making sketches in a little book, while the others chattered and occasionally looked at what he was doing when he exclaimed at a specially interesting specimen.

He delighted in recommending to his friends books such as the History of Selborne by the Hampshire naturalist parson Gilbert White, the ornithological books of Bewick, and others that detailed the creatures of the region and plantings of the seasons; and he earnestly adjured every one to compare these notes with the natural productions.

Henry had a keen interest in all that he could learn from Charles, and Catherine, with her enthusiasm for every enthusiasm of her husband's, was not far behind; and if Sarah cared not much more for nature beyond picking flowers, she was happy to pick them in the company of Mr. Speedwell.

Contrary to the usual way of things, it was the evenings, supposed to be passed in gaieties in Assembly Rooms and concerts, that were unproductive of happiness. The knowledge that the scandal was the exact sort that the gossips relished most, was inescapable. And worse was to come, for it was soon on every tongue that Lord Craven and Harriette had actually gone off together, and he was supposed to have taken her to his country shooting box, Ashdown Park in Berkshire.

"It is the prettiest place," Sarah, reported to the others. "My friends Amelia and Louisa, have the whole story. Ashdown is about forty miles from here, and like a little jewel box, but it is very remote, quite in the middle of the countryside, so they wonder if there will be any thing to amuse Miss Harriette."

"There will be Lord Craven, I collect," said Henry dryly.

"But what people are wondering is, will Captain Tilney follow her, and fight a duel?"

"Frederick will not trouble himself to do any such thing, I can assure you. He will have some body new before Miss Harriette ceases being a byword in Bath."

Mr. Speedwell looked concerned, and Catherine was not altogether surprised when he presented himself at the Allens' lodgings early on the morning after this conversation, and announced with regret that he was come to bid farewell. He did not seem at ease, was not his usual open and sociable self, and his excuses for his departure appeared unconvincing to his hearers. He seemed of all things unable to look at Sarah, but kept his eyes on the floor.

"My father is not wishing to remain in Bath any longer," he explained, "he is not convinced that the waters are doing him good, and I must immediately escort him home, back into Kent."

"But you will return?" Sarah asked eagerly, "Once he is settled?" She seemed to have no inkling of what was to befall her, and waited hopefully for an answer. It was not the one she wanted.

"I fear it will not be in my power," was all he said, and after wishing health and happiness to all the party, he left with some abruptness.

Sarah went into her room to weep, to the surprise of no one.

"Your poor sister," Eleanor murmured to Catherine. "I am so sorry for her disappointment, and all the more as it is directly owing to Frederick's behavior."

Catherine could not conceal her own distress. "She likes Mr. Speedwell so much," she said, "we all do, for that. It is such a pity. Do you really think he will not come back?"

"He said he would not," Henry reminded her. "His family may have ordered him to remove himself from a family of such reputation, and after such a display, who can blame him. It is really too bad."

"I am afraid Sarah's heart will be broken."

Henry thought for a few moments. "Catherine, it is nearly time for us to be returning to Woodston. Suppose we ask Sarah to accompany us? It might be a distraction for her, and we may be able to offer her some comfort."

Catherine agreed, and was grateful for his kindness. Sarah at first did not care where she went, but after being gently pressed by her sister on the subject, considered that she would rather be with Catherine than any where else. Certainly the gay scenes of Bath would be oppressive now, and she never wanted to set eyes on that nasty Captain Tilney ever again.

The parting with the Easthams was sad, but they were all glad they had had the chance to spend so much time together, and the memory of that would always be very precious.

Chapter Sixteen

"How glad I am to get *home*," said Catherine with emphasis, as their own pretty house came into view. "Oh look! The hollyhocks have grown so! And here come the dear dogs."

She was encouraged that Sarah brightened up at seeing the parsonage, and admired both house and gardens, as much as her lack of spirits would allow. The drawing-room itself, which Catherine had once called "the prettiest room in England," was the first object of her notice. She looked about in open admiration.

"Why! You said it was pretty, and no mistake! I never saw any thing like those lovely long windows, and the apple-trees ripening so beautifully! Oh! I should like to wander among them."

"And so you shall," promised Catherine.

Despite the recent rending events, the travels, the shocks, and the sadnesses, the young Tilneys soon felt almost as if they had never left Woodston at all. The summer weather continued golden and delightful, with the sweet strawberries reddening, and Catherine was in the garden more than half the day, pruning plants, and learning to tell what were weeds. Henry, with whom botany was become an absorbing interest, was glad to provide pleasant instruction on this subject as well as all others within his ken, but to his credit, none that were outside of it.

Catherine did not lose sight of her object in encouraging Sarah to be out in the garden as often as might be, or taking exercise by walking in the country lanes about Woodston; but it was uphill work, for her sister would persist in adverting very often to the late events at Bath. At tea time especially she would talk of nothing else.

"Was it not shocking, Catherine, at Bath, how the name of Northanger Abbey was on every tongue? Even before you arrived, every one was agog about the place! It was so odd, to know it to be connected with myself."

"Northanger Abbey! Why, I did not know that the place itself was under discussion at Bath," said Henry, mystified.

"Oh yes, from the time of your late father's death, you know," Sarah told him.

"But why, I wonder? An old man's death, even if unexpected and perhaps by questionable means, hardly could amount to much of a story in Bath. Depend upon it, Bath only takes notice of scandal. Elopings, jiltings, alliances – that sort of thing. Am I not right in that, Sarah? Bath loves a sensation."

"So it does. But all the gossips called it a murder, and said that Northanger was become a hotbed of wickedness, immorality, and mayhem. News of the General's death, and then, coming so soon after that, Frederick's behavior, carried from one end of the town to the other. And you see what was the result."

She looked sad again, and Catherine remarked, "I am sure that people in Bath will soon forget all about events up in Gloucestershire. It is quite a distance."

"It was Captain Tilney's arrival, on quitting Northanger for Bath, that caused the worst mischief," Sarah said in a low tone, "and that, I think, will not be so soon forgot."

"His bringing that Harriette – Wilson, I suppose she must be called - with him, certainly did set the town on its ear," Henry concluded, shaking his head. "I warned him, but Frederick could never be told any thing, and so that was that."

"I don't know how he could like a ruined woman." Sarah dropped her chin on her hands pensively.

"Dear Sarah," chided Catherine, in an elder-sister way, "an unmarried girl like you ought not think about such things. It is a shame. Have some tea, and try not to think about it."

"It is not me who is the shame, and I can hardly help knowing what was known to every one in Bath."

"The shame is the talk about our family. To have it blazoned in Bath, is as bad as seeing it in newspapers," said Catherine.

"They print stories like that every day," Henry observed, "about matrimonial partings, and duels, along with the comings and goings of notables. Lord Craven is not likely to escape a line about his new liaison, though I hope Frederick may be overlooked."

"Your brother does not seem to care if he is talked about or not," said Sarah, "associating with a demi-rep."

"Oh, Sarah, language," reproved Catherine half-heartedly.

"That is Bath," Henry told her with a shrug. "Any girl learns about the world very quickly there. You see for yourself."

"Well, shocking as it is, Henry, let us hope for the best. With Miss Harriette gone off now, perhaps Frederick will now reform, and lead a decent life from now on."

A faint noise from Henry, which might have been a snort.

"He may come to a greater realizing sense of his responsibilities," Catherine continued hopefully.

"You may as well talk of a realizing weasel," said Henry. "I dislike having to speak thus of my brother, but he has always been susceptible to some woman or other, and has but an indifferent conscience."

"I am more than ever thankful he did not made overtures to you, Sarah."

"Do you think I would have encouraged him if he did?" she retorted with spirit.

"Not much danger of that, young women of virtue are not what attracts my brother," said Henry, dryly.

"There is no telling who he will turn up with next," Catherine sighed.

"Now, look here, girls," said Henry briskly. "It would be a positive indulgence to my feelings, if we did not discuss Frederick any longer. I hope he is very happy in Bath, and will contrive to behave himself; and that is the last I will say on the subject."

"It will be better for you, too, Sarah, not to dwell on Bath overmuch," advised Catherine, remembering her own mother's long-ago advice to her, in a not dissimilar situation, when she had been pining over what she had thought the loss of Henry.

"Yes. Now that Sarah is here, there are the gardens and the poultry for her to enjoy, and also our more rational pursuits in the evenings. We can have some good reading to divert and entertain her."

"Reading?" asked Sarah with an almost visible gape.

"Oh yes, we are reading a new novel by Walter Scott," said Catherine enthusiastically. "So beautiful, all about Scotland. I cannot stop listening, and Henry does read so very well."

"That will be very nice," said Sarah faintly.

"Oh! Don't use that word, Sarah. Henry does not like it. Look here, I am glad we have some of these little muffins with our tea and strawberries. Our cook does make them so very well, and I put up the damson jam myself."

"Thank you, Catherine," said Sarah, consoling herself with a warm and buttery muffin.

Bath gradually receded into the distance in their conversations, and their outdoor pursuits helped to keep it out of mind. The weather was midsummer perfection, with roses abloom and bees and butterflies attending them, and the young people were happy with their gardening, some cottage-visiting, and taking lessons from the tolerant cook. Every evening there was reading as Henry proposed, for the house boasted many books in Henry's fine library, though his only regret about summer was that the evenings were so short and the days so long they could not get through the books at a winter's pace.

With such pleasant occupation, Sarah improved visibly, not reaching so high as the blessing of happy spirits, but less drooping and sad. Catherine was pleased with her sister's progress, and also by that of her laden fruit trees, and perhaps with the blossoming of her world in general. She had begun to entertain some secret hopes that she had not yet confided in her husband, but resolved that she soon would.

Henry seemed to guess what she would say through her very looks; and they exchanged many secret smiles, while he waited for her to be certain, and to speak. If Henry minded not having Catherine's undivided society at this time, he never said so; and both took satisfaction in that Sarah seemed to be feeling at home, returning to cheerfulness, and to have some enjoyment in watching the blithe honeymoon summer idyll that obtained week after week at Woodston.

Into this beatitude, the Tilneys in their garden were surprised to see a carriage turn into their sweep, promising a new set of visitors to the parsonage, whose inhabitants were not in truth looking for any. With some perturbation Henry discerned the arms and livery of the Northanger carriage itself.

"We are in for a visit from Frederick, I collect," he told Catherine.

"Frederick? Here? And just when we have been having some success in making Sarah forget about all that," Catherine lamented.

"I can't imagine what on earth would make him come calling," said Henry. "He despises our domesticity, and our dull little parsonage, as he once rather offensively called it."

"Really, he does seem to have strong opinions about marriage altogether."

"Yes, he says it is an insipid institution."

"I have always wondered, Henry, how you happened to have such a brother. With the same parents, how can your influences have been so very different? Not only your characters, but your opinions and your morals, bear hardly a resemblance to each other."

"Ah, well, he was always my father's favorite, you see, and generally obeyed his dictates. I think the only subject of disagreement they ever had was about Frederick's marriage."

"There is someone with him. A young lady. Who can it be?" asked Sarah.

"I expect that we are about to have our wish of seeing who Frederick will have taken up with next," said Henry.

"Who indeed," said Catherine. "I fear that, whoever she is, if she is driving with Frederick, she must be indifferent to her own reputation. But we shall see."

When the carriage pulled up, and Frederick jumped down to hand the reins to the groom, he then gave his hand to help his companion. What was the astonishment of the home party to see that the lady who came towards them, beaming an artificial smile beneath her fashionable ostrich-feathered bonnet, was none other than Isabella Thorpe.

Chapter Seventeen

"Catherine my love!" Isabella shrieked as she jumped down and ran to her former friend, feathers flying, as Frederick followed leisurely in her wake.

"Is it really you, Isabella!" exclaimed Catherine, truly surprised but not best pleased. "How do you happen to be here? You and Captain Tilney are not –"

"Engaged? Oh no, not yet, are we Frederick, but it is only a formality after all," said Isabella carelessly. "Well! You did not praise Woodston too highly at all, I must say. It is quite the pretty little cottage. Small, but attractive, if you like that sort of thing."

"It is a parsonage," corrected Catherine, rather hurt, "and it is a very good size for one."

"If you say so. It does look very nearly like a gentleman's residence, and I have no doubt will have room enough to house us both. We are on our way to Northanger Abbey, and thought we might break our journey here."

"But how can you be traveling together, if you are not married, or at least engaged?" Catherine objected, scandalized.

"Don't be a goose, Catherine. You must learn that I am Captain Tilney's lady as surely as if the banns had been read, and you need not trouble yourself about the proprieties. Prudishness does not suit a young married woman such as yourself."

"Frederick, I regret having to say this, but you must be aware that it is not permissable for a man's mistress to be received in a parsonage – unless perchance she is seeking sanctuary; but that hardly seems to be the case here. It is not in our power to entertain such a couple under this roof."

"Oh, do have some common sense, Henry. I am thinking only of getting a good night's rest on my way back to Northanger," replied Frederick crossly, "nothing more; and I beg to point out that Miss Thorpe is not at all cut from the same cloth as that little baggage Harriette. You would be perfectly within your rights to deny your door to her, for you were right about what she was. I will even go so far as to acknowledge that I should have known better about her. You saw that she was off with the first lord who propositioned her at Bath. Fifteen! She has the cunning of fifty."

"Well, but don't talk of other girls," Isabella pouted. "You may be sure I, at least, shall never abandon you, my beloved."

"Then you shall be a most remarkable and unprecedented sort of woman, my dear."

"But Frederick, seriously, surely you see that if you are traveling with Miss Thorpe without benefit of matrimony, it is no different than living with Harriette Wilson."

"The idea!" cried Isabella indignantly. "How can you name me in the same breath as that sort of creature!"

"Yes," agreed Frederick, "you had better mind how you speak of Miss Thorpe, Henry. She is no woman of the town, or anything of that nature. Isabella is a lady, a respectable young woman of good family, just as much as your own wife, and for that matter she is your own wife's very good friend. She deserves no less than common respect."

Henry bowed. "I certainly will respect Miss Thorpe, if I can, but the principle remains fixed. Whatever the world countenances, we must not receive an unlawful mistress, here at the parsonage, whatever their family origins. It is not in our remit to overlook immorality."

"Immorality? And you would forbid us your house for that? exclaimed Frederic, incensed. "How do you dare to do that, little brother! Try and see if you will retain visiting privileges at Northanger Abbey!"

"Really, your husband is awfully uncivil," Isabella drawled, turning to Catherine. "And me practically your oldest friend in the world – your first in Bath, and the sharer of so many pleasures! Have not we been reading and promenading together, and practically being bosom sisters? Yet here you are, countenancing your husband preaching to such a friend! I would not have believed it possible. Such unkindness, when a woman who will be my own sister-in-law, would turn me out! It is enough to make one positively weep." She dabbed at her dry eyes.

"No," returned Henry. "It is not our purpose to turn you out, Miss Thorpe, I assure you. If you will only quit your unlawful situation, you shall be welcomed with all kindness and consideration. A comfortable home will be found for you, if you choose not to return to your mother, though that is what I would advise."

Isabella scouted this suggestion with scorn. "Really, Mr. Tilney, I will not even deign to consider such a suggestion. The idea of my leaving my dear Captain Tilney, my affianced husband-presumptive! Why, do you not realize, soon I shall be the mistress of Northanger Abbey. Then you will be sorry you spoke to me in such a manner. But I can be generous, even if you cannot, and still assure you that when Frederick and I are wed, we shall look forward to having many happy family house parties at the Abbey."

"We would hardly care to visit it," said Catherine indignantly.

"Hark to your little wife," laughed Frederick, raising his heavy eyebrows in surprise. "What spirit! And here I thought she was a mealy-mouthed girl enough."

"If that is your opinion, I wonder you stopped to visit us," said Henry with some heat.

"What do you know, I see somebody else coming to visit," spoke up Sarah unexpectedly. "Another carriage – no, it is a curricle. The man in it is driving awfully fast. Goodness, look at him whip that horse! He must be a horrid man."

Isabella turned her head to look. "Curricle? Well, I declare! It is my own brother, John! Look, Catherine, do you see? How pleased you must be, for he was once quite your beau."

"He never was my beau, and I am not pleased to see him," spoke up Catherine, angrily. "What can he mean by this intrusion?"

"I am sure he will tell us," pointed out Henry dryly. "John Thorpe never kept quiet for two minutes together, and you may depend upon it, with such an opportunity as this, talk he will."

Thorpe was heard hallooing as he turned into the sweep, and heavily descended from his equipage.

"Hullo Isabella! Are you surprised to see me? How d'ye do, Tilney – Captain Tilney too – and here is my sweet little Catherine, Mrs. Tilney now, how strange that sounds! I conceive you must be sorry you did not marry me, are you not? You don't see such a curricle as mine every day, and here you are settled in a poky little parsonage far from every thing good that's going on."

"I am sorry our house does not meet with your approval, Mr. Thorpe," said Henry coldly. "Perhaps this may tend to make your visit short. And to what do we owe the honour?"

"Invite me inside for tea, will you, or better yet, something stronger. A pint of ale – it is so cursedly hot, and I have been racing all this way. I am on a very important mission that cannot possibly be delayed," he said importantly.

"Very well then, in that case you had better have your man groom your horse at once, she is all lathered," directed Henry. "I wonder you can drive her so recklessly. It is cruelty."

"Reckless! Cruel! I! Why I am one of the finest horsemen in the kingdom – your own father, General Tilney, once told me so, I'll know you know. Yes he did. 'Thorpe,' he said, 'I have been at many races, and known many riders of the highest skill with the highest bred horses, but you rank among the best of the lot.'"

"My father took care of his horses," said Frederick contemptuously, "and did not lavish idle insincere compliments. I am with Henry here, and do not believe a word of it."

"Sir! You doubt my word? My friendship with General Tilney was a proverb for warmth, and intimacy, and all that sort of thing. Why, he trusted me with his plans, and his business, countless times, don't you know."

"Then perhaps you know something about his death," put in Henry.

"I? Bless me, no, how would I know that? It is said in Bath that he was killed, murdered someway, by a Frenchman; but I was not within a hundred miles of the place when it happened, I assure you."

"No one suspected you, Thorpe," said Henry, "but now tell us what is your business here, and do it quickly or I shall lose patience."

"What a way to talk to the man who has your brother's best interests at heart, and has taken so much trouble to find him."

"Find Captain Tilney?" asked Catherine, puzzled. "But he was at Bath. Could not you have found him there, and settled your business without coming out of the way to Woodston?"

"As clear thinking a mind as any girl in the kingdom," Thorpe exclaimed. "I always did admire your good thinking, and good nature, upon my word. And to be sure, you are blooming – I hope you have expectations of a little one, or else Tilney here is not doing his job."

Catherine was silenced, pink in the face.

"As a matter of fact, I reached Bath too late – only to be told that this fine Captain Tilney had carried my sister off to Northanger Abbey."

"You were told that at Bath?" asked Henry.

"Yes; it was common knowledge. Every one was talking. I'll have you know that your brother has made my sister the talk of the town. Laying bets as to whether he will marry her or not, or if she was on the road to ruin, like la belle Harriette. Well, I could not let that kind of talk about my sister pass, so I hared off after the eloping couple, and reached Northanger Abbey in the shortest amount of time the journey ever was made, I daresay."

"You went to Northanger?"

"To be sure I did. That's how my horse here got lathered up so finely, as you observe. I came tearing into the Abbey at the finest speed ever seen, absolutely unmatched, only to be told, of all things, that the master was believed to be at Woodston, for he certainly was not at home."

"Who could have thought he was at Woodston?" Catherine wondered.

"Oh, all the servants. They talk too, just as much as folks at Bath, and they thought if I wanted to find the erring pair, I must come here. So that's what I have done."

"And to what purpose?" asked Henry.

"Why, to talk sense into this silly girl Belle. I won't allow you disgrace our family, you know, sister. That would be a step too far. My mother would be shocked at you turning mistress to the captain, and never hold up her head again. And my sisters would never catch husbands, that's flat, so it's a very serious matter. I'm never going to support them, I promise you that. There's money at stake here; but you never think of consequences, do you? So you see, you must do the right thing."

"I am perfectly willing," Isabella fluttered her eyelashes at Captain Tilney, "but it is my intended whom you must persuade into action."

"If he is your intended, there can't be much argument, then," said her brother, satisfied. "He has promised, has he?"

Captain Tilney shrugged. "I intend to take Isabella to Northanger Abbey, for company, and then we will see."

"Why, that is no answer at all, Captain. If I don't get a better one, there will be a breach of promise suit at the least, I assure you, and more than likely it will end with my having to horsewhip you!"

"I'd like to see you try it," said Frederick calmly, towering over the corpulent Thorpe.

"Well – I hope I can trust you, that's all," said Thorpe, subsiding.

"I mean no harm to Isabella, that's all I will say," returned Frederick.

"I have it," said Thorpe, snapping his fingers. "I know what."

"Mercy, what?" exclaimed Catherine.

"Why, I'll accompany you to Northanger, that's what I'll do. That way, Belle will be properly chaperoned, her name won't be ruined, and I'll be able to witness the wedding. It will be killing two birds with one stone. Then I can pay a nice long wedding-visit at Northanger, where I am quite sure you will set a better table than the pitiful parsonage here is likely to do."

There was a stupefied silence. Then Henry, after a moment's thought said, "If that is your decision, Mr. Thorpe, you may be encouraged in it. It is undeniable that you are the properest person to protect your sister, and to witness her nuptials."

"I wish you would come too, Catherine," pleaded Isabella. "I will hold you to your promise. Don't you recollect, you always said you would be at my wedding?"

Catherine was lost for an answer, since she had certainly once promised to be at Isabella's wedding, but that was when she was to marry her brother. The audaciousness of Isabella's transferring this invitation to her marriage to another man, was such a piece of presumption, she did not know what to say.

"No, I think Mr. Thorpe will be sufficient escort," Henry decided, "and if the men have watered your horse, you had best be on your way, as it wants only a few hours of sunset."

"Oh, curses, I can make it to Northanger in under two hours flat," Thorpe objected, "but Tilney's carriage is another story. What a sad thing it is, the master of Northanger drive such a rattletrip, he should be ashamed. But I've no objection to being off, so as soon as you can be ready, Belle."

Chapter Eighteen

Relieved at the felicitous departure of their visitors, the young Tilneys and Sarah were only too relieved to return to their pleasant occupations. Good weather continued to shine upon a succession of glorious midsummer days, so that Catherine learnt to discern a chequered skipper butterfly at ten yards, and to no longer confuse bulbs with onions. Their reading proceeded apace, too, and even Sarah found interest in listening to Henry's books, and watching his and Catherine's mutual joy in their studies.

It was not long before their home peace was broken by another intrusion, however, and of an alarming nature.

Henry was reading to Catherine and Sarah from Mrs. Burney's new novel *Camilla,* and they were exchanging opinions.

"I don't know why Mr. Thorpe despised this novel so much," said Catherine, "I think it is most entertaining. I cannot wait to hear what happens next!"

"I doubt he really read it," said Henry. "He does not strike me as someone who would have patience for three volumes entire."

"I have always wanted to read it, partly because of his telling me it was such nonsense; I doubted it, as Miss Burney is so very fine an author, and acclaimed by so many. And I could not help suspecting that any thing Mr. Thorpe likes, I would not, and vice versa."

Henry laughed, and wondered how far Mr. Thorpe had got in the book.

"Why, I can make a very good guess as to that. He said it was about nothing at all but an old man playing at see-saw and learning Latin; and that happens, you know, in the third chapter. That must have been where he put it down."

"But that is perfectly ridiculous of him," said Sarah. That chapter, when poor Sir Hugh drops Eugenia and she is injured, is the most desperate scene of all! How could any one stop reading then? And then she gets smallpox, and Sir Hugh leaves her his fortune – oh! I do love it."

"You are a young woman of taste, and I am glad you are enjoying Camilla, as indeed, so am I," Henry told her. "But I think I know what John Thorpe's true objection to the book was."

"What?" asked both girls.

"Don't you see the similarity of poor Sir Hugh to himself? Unlearned, uninformed, a rattle who always veers to senseless extremes in his opinions and causes endless mischief – it must have discomfited Mr.

Thorpe very much, to meet with such a portrait as that."

"How true, Henry. I do see the similarity. Only, you know, though he was very ignorant and silly, Sir Hugh had at least a good heart."

"And there the resemblance ends," agreed Henry. He would have said more, but the discussion was interrupted by a servant knocking rapidly at the door; and the next moment he ushered in a flurried woman, who rushed into the drawing-room. It was Isabella Thorpe, heated and disheveled, her eyes wide with distress.

"Why Isabella!" cried Catherine as they all rose. "What has happened? Are you ill?"

"I don't know," sobbed Isabella, falling into a chair. The others could see her exhaustion as well as the dirt crusting her skirts, and her muddy torn slippers.

"Have you come from Northanger Abbey, Miss Thorpe?" Henry asked, "How did you arrive here?"

"You can't have walked all this way, though your poor slippers look like it," said Catherine.

"Yes I did!"

"But it is twenty miles! How could you!"

"I am very footsore," and Isabella showed her swollen feet in the burst slippers.

"I should say! Oh, Isabella, you must have hurt yourself. You must rest, and bathe, at once," and Catherine gave orders to the maids to prepare a room, a washtub and clean clothes for the poor traveler.

"Now tell us, while we wait for the things to be readied, what has happened, Isabella. Do not be afraid," for Isabella was most uncharacteristically trembling as if in fear.

"Oh, I simply cannot tell you. It is all too dreadful."

"Go on, Miss Thorpe. You are safe here, with us."

"Mr. Tilney, you will be shocked to know it. It is your brother. He has gone mad!"

"What, Frederick? But surely that is not likely, Miss Thorpe. Whatever you may think of his character, Frederick has a very cool head, and is too sufficiently master of himself to be suspected of being mad. Why do you say he is so?"

"Any man can be mad, Mr. Tilney, if he is drinking enough!" she cried.

"I can't contradict that," agreed Henry, "and Frederick does like a drink as well as the next man; but still, he never has been a toper, or given to much excess in his drinking. What had he been drinking, to produce such an effect? It is not much like him."

"Why, he has inherited your father's cellar, you know, and he ordered up some of his best and oldest bottles – some Venetian wine, very rare and ancient, I think he said. He offered me some but I would not have it. I could barely look at him, I was too angry."

"And why were you angry?"

"I think we quarreled almost every moment since arriving at Northanger Abbey," said Isabella tearfully, her lips trembling.

"What started this? What caused these quarrels?"

"It was mostly the marrying thing, Mr. Tilney, to say the truth," Isabelle sighed, and combed her fingers through her matted damp hair. "My brother left Northanger in a terrible rage because he could not bring Frederick to the point of offering for me, no matter what he said: indeed, the more John argued, the more Frederick resisted. After he was gone, Frederick called me a shrew and a nag from a worthless family, and said he never would marry me while he had free will. Then he started drinking that horrid wine, which I think has poisoned him and made him mad."

"Poisoned! And his father was poisoned!" exclaimed Catherine, and she and Henry shared a concerned glance at one another.

"And when he was in that state, he started to beat me, with a stick he kept for the purpose," Isabella confessed with shame, "but luckily he was so fuddled and sick from the drink that I was able to run away. I ran for hours through the forest, hardly stopping for rest, and drinking from the streams; and here I am!"

Her appearance corroborated her story, and Henry and Catherine regarded her with pity as well as horror.

"Oh, how I wish I had never seen him! I wish I had never gone to Northanger with him! Oh! I might have listened to you, Mr. Tilney, you were right, and such wickedness did not answer."

She sobbed, and Henry told his wife, "I believe she is really repentant. We must help her."

"Yes, we must, indeed," said Catherine, "this is so very shocking. Do not worry, Isabella, we will see what is to be done with Frederick, and meanwhile you are perfectly safe here."

The servants reported the room ready and Catherine rose. "Come, you shall make yourself comfortable, and think no more of this tonight."

"But what if Frederick comes for me?" asked Isabella, wide eyed and trembling with fright, looking as different a picture of her bold, assured former self as could possibly be imagined.

"He will not," said Henry with certainty. "Judging from what you describe as his state, he cannot, to begin with; and here we have men to guard you, and Catherine and Sarah and the servants to nurse you. You are safe. I shall ride over to Northanger tonight, myself, to inspect the situation there, and to remonstrate with Frederick."

"Oh, Henry! Must you?"

"I believe so. Do not be anxious, Catherine, I will take Thomas with me, and we will see to Frederick. This behavior is so unlike him, I believe Miss Thorpe may be correct, and he is suffering an illness, perhaps from what he has imbibed."

"Oh Henry, you will be careful!"

Henry gave her the warmest assurances, and departed in haste on the road to Northanger.

Chapter Nineteen

For two days Catherine remained in the most direful suspense, unsure if Henry was safe at his old home, or if Frederick might still be in a violent and dangerous state. Sarah could not offer any opinion, and Isabella had no power or spirit to tell any more than what she had told already.

On the third day the coachman returned with a letter from Northanger and Catherine's fear was half abated as she recognized Henry's writing, but the contents of the letter were not of a tendency to reassure her.

"My dearest wife,"

he wrote,

"I am reluctant to write of what must alarm you, at such a time as my being away from home, but rest at least in knowing that I am well, and in no personal difficulty or discomfort. My brother's situation is, however, I regret to say, very dangerous indeed, for he is extremely ill. Miss Thorpe's information was correct, for by observation, and by talking to the servants, I have concluded that his illness is indeed due to a most virulent form of alcohol poisoning, evidently from taking too much of one of my father's venomous foreign wines. He is indeed in a state that must be called mad. The doctor is with him, and he confirms my fears as to Frederick's symptoms, but is unable to alleviate them by any physic, nor does he give any hope of the patient's recovery.

The poison has penetrated too far into his system, and he is now confined to his bed, the same that was my father's so short a time ago. He has terrible imaginings, and his raving cries are piteous; he insists that he is being tormented by ghosts and demons who are punishing him for his sins. I cannot tell if he repents of the worst of them, though they include cruel mistreatment of his servants, which I hear about from all sides; and of course the bringing of his mistresses into the house. His abuse of Miss Thorpe corresponds with her statement, but in a quieter moment he has spoken to ask where she is, and I take this as evidence that he does not think entirely unfeelingly of her.

Catherine, I must ask you to do something, if you can feel yourself strong enough; and if you have any fears of the journey for your health, do not give it another thought, and I will contrive some other way. However, it would be most expedient, if you were able to bring Miss Thorpe back to Northanger. I could then endeavor to bring about and consecrate her marriage with Frederick, before it is too late, so that he does not die with this sin on his soul, nor that she should live on with it.

I have sent Thomas back with the curricle, and after he has changed horses (I think the young cob is in the best state for the journey, for the bay needs rest), and you have packed the things you will need, you and Miss Thorpe might set out this afternoon. The curricle is in good repair, and certainly safe enough to draw you comfortably the distance. Thomas is getting on a bit but he is trustworthy and steady-handed so I feel at ease with him taking care of you. The three hours' journey should bring you hither before darkness falls. The weather is dry so I am not afraid of your being caught in a shower; Thomas has undertaken the journey twice lately, so he is thoroughly familiar with the five miles' route to the main turnpike and then the turning that takes the road through the forest to the Northanger gates.

My Catherine, I look forward greatly to seeing you before darkness falls, and together we can put things to rights here in this unfortunate mansion that I used to call home.
Your ever loving husband,
H. Tilney"

Catherine, though concerned and apprehensive, did not hesitate, but began to give orders for the carriage to be readied, and clothes packed for what she hoped would be no long stay at Northanger. Preparations were fairly advanced, and she had good hopes of departing in as timely a manner as Henry desired, but she was startled to come up against the obstacle of Isabella's utter refusal to go.

Her inquiry as to what extra clothing Isabella might need to bring with her, linens or a borrowed cloak, she thought a mere matter of form, but Isabella's reply was as prompt as it was adamant.

"I will not go back to Northanger. Don't think it, Catherine. I have vowed never to go back to that dreadful place, and no more I will."

"But Isabella – I told you what Henry has written. Poor Frederick is ill, just as you described, and likely to die. You have a chance to make your union lawful, and to right your position, while he is still alive. Do you not want to clear your conscience, and your name?"

"It could not help my conscience to be married to a beast, Catherine. And what if he does not die? I should find myself well and truly trapped!"

Catherine was perplexed. "The doctor and Henry think Frederick has no chance of survival," she advanced.

"Oh phoo, Catherine! It is always such people who live for ever, and I assure you I do not intend to be tied to such a man for life. Beatings do not agree with me and I won't stand them, whatever you say."

"No one will treat you in such a way, Isabella! If Frederick should by some chance survive, and become violent, why, terrible though it would be, he would undoubtedly need to be confined. Do not have fear. We would see to it that you are perfectly safe, and not ill treated in any way."

"It's not within reason to make such a promise. What if he got loose, and killed me! You and Henry would not be there to be his gaolers all the time."

"Where do you get such fantastic ideas, Isabella! Consider that, if you are married, you will be assured of a respectable position, all your life."

"But you don't understand. Do you not know, I thought you did know, that there is a terrible curse upon that house, and most especially upon the wife of the oldest son. If I marry Frederick, it will surely mean a terrible death. He told me the whole story himself. Why should I marry him and suffer a ghastly fate? Better to be living and sinful, than dead and cursed!"

"Now, Isabella, do talk sense. I know we read of such things in horrid stories, when we were girls amusing ourselves together in Bath; but curses are not real! You need Henry to remind you that this is the nineteenth century, it is England, and there are no phantoms and monsters. Surely, you know all that as well as I do!"

"Perhaps I do, Catherine, but only recollect what kind of a history the Tilney family has had at Northanger. Every wife of the oldest son of the house has met a terrible and premature death; and be it a curse or not, it is still too direful a hazard. I will not take the chance. Could you do it? Would you have married your Henry if he had been the oldest son? Answer me that."

"Yes, I would," said Catherine stoutly, "for it is all nothing but nonsense. The way to end such a chain of circumstances is to act rationally. And, Isabella, it could only be for your own good that you marry Frederick. It will make you an honest and respectable woman. To reform your practices, and enter into a good Christian marriage, is to do what is right. A sinful life does not answer. Surely you already see that."

"Catherine, you do not hear me at all," Isabella retorted, exasperated. "What if, after you and Henry leave, he continues to misuse and maltreat me? Quite aside from curses, the Tilney men have not always been famous for treating their wives kindly, and you know very well that a wife has no recourse in such a case. She is entirely her husband's property. Who is there to protect me?"

"The law would protect you," Catherine said firmly. "It does, in extreme cases like this; and depend upon it, Henry and I would always see that justice was done. Then, too, Isabella, I dislike mentioning it, but it may carry some weight with you, that as either Captain Tilney's wife or his widow, you would be the possessor of considerable means of your own, and might put protection for yourself in place."

"That's true enough," Isabella said, considering. "You know that money concerns are nothing to me – I have not a mercenary bone in my body, and think fortune hunting the most vulgar thing imaginable. Just so I have a sufficiency, I look for no more. Captain Tilney has inherited a very considerable fortune, however." She looked thoughtful.

"To be sure he has," said Catherine, "and no one would call you mercenary for attending to the security of your situation; it is only prudent. And only think of the relief it will be to you, to be able to enter into decent society again. You do not wish to live your life as an outcast, surely! But that is the punishment that society imposes in such cases, upon women."

"Yes, you are right there. I had not really thought of such things. And as for the danger – why, if I accompany you to Northanger, there will be yourself, and Henry, and the servants – I would not be in immediate jeopardy, at any rate, and am not forced to marry Frederick if I decide against it, after all, am I?."

"Certainly not. You can judge of what his state is, and if he has come to his better self. Henry and the doctor can both advise you, as to what is the right thing to do."

"Very well, then, Catherine, I will go with you," Isabella made up her mind reluctantly.

Chapter Twenty

The Woodston road was both familiar and pretty, and Catherine's spirits were much uplifted by the thought that she was on her way to her own Henry. She was sure the journey would do her no harm, despite her expectant state, for Henry's carriage was as comfortable and well-hung as possible, and they had often been taking drives about the countryside since she had informed him of the joy that was to befall them. Now she happily recalled those drives taken on this very road together, and pointed out cottages and fields, hills and flowers to Isabella, who did not, in point of fact, seem to be listening.

The main turnpike road was good, though less interesting, and the carriage made rapid time. The sun was hot and halfway through the journey the coachman suggested they stop to rest the horse in a shady lay-by at the start of the forest road, and eat their cold chicken, bread and cheese. He thoughtfully sat on one side of a large bowlder, and the ladies sat on the other.

After a reasonable rest, and some cold tea, they resumed their seats in the curricle, which now turned onto the forest path.

The trees were thick, and the horse had to pick its way more slowly along the path, where the light was fading.

"Goodness, Thomas is a pokey driver," complained Isabella, growing tired of the uncomfortable bumps the carriage made on the forest road, worse than on the turnpike. "I declare it is growing dark already, we shall be in pitch blackness by the time we reach Northanger."

"No such thing," Catherine said encouragingly, "it is high summer, and does not grow full dark till at least nine. We want at least two hours of that now, I am sure."

"We are a little slow, I am afraid, ma'am," said Thomas, turning round on his box. "We was a little delayed getting away, and it is hard picking our way through these here trees. But we will do it, and before full dark."

"Humph!" said Isabella. "We can expect to spend the night in the open, I am sure."

"Don't think such dreadful things, Isabella. Thomas knows the way and we are certain to be safe."

At that moment they heard a crashing through the trees, that sounded like a runaway horse. The girls clung to each other, startled. "Hey!" shouted Thomas, shaking his whip to warn the oncoming creature away. But instead of turning, as they expected, it charged right at them, and Catherine and Isabella had a glimpse of foamy mouth, and madly glowing red eyes, as it came rushing onwards.

Isabella screamed. "Oh, what is it Catherine?"

"Hold tight, Isabella!"

"That is no steed – that is a goblin! No, I swear it is a Gytrash! Have you read of them?"

"What on earth do you mean? Do be quiet, Isabella – it has run away but is only a horse – "

"Get down!" shouted Thomas in his loudest voice, as the animal reared on its hind legs and came down on their own horse, overturning the carriage completely. Then it went crashing away into the woods.

Isabella did not stop screaming for an instant, but Catherine, who was in the upper position, scrabbled to try to open the door, which was above her. "Oh do be still for a moment, Isabella – are you hurt?"

"I am sure I am crushed from the way you are lying on me. Do get off. My door is on the ground, cannot you open yours?"

"I believe it will take both of us to do it. Thomas! Thomas! Can you not help?"

The coachman was silent.

"Oh he must be dead," despaired Isabella. "And the horse. What shall we do?"

"Do not say such things, Isabella. Do not think them. Come, put your hands here, and let us both lift up at once – "

The uppermost door lifted up, and Catherine, smudged and dusty, managed to clamber out. Sitting on the side of the coach, she reached down her arm to pull Isabella up, and soon the girls were sitting on the side of the coach.

"The horse is down, and I don't see Thomas," said Catherine, concerned.

"Perhaps the Gytrash has got them."

"Don't be silly, what are you talking of? What is a gytrash?"

"Oh, don't you know, they are creatures, dogs or horses, who haunt lonely roads and lead travelers astray. I read of them in some book or other about ghosts. I am sure that thing was one; did you not see how red his eyes were?"

"Never mind, poor beast," said Catherine, not without a shudder. "I think I can slide down easily enough, it is not too high to do so, and the ground is soft. If I do it, will you try to follow?"

The maneuver was done with success, and the girls stood in the road, shaken but unhurt. Walking around to the front of the carriage, they saw that sure enough the horse was down, and whinnying in pain from what looked like a broken foreleg. Beside him lay Thomas.

Catherine knelt beside him, and examining him, shook his shoulder gently. The man was breathing, and presently opened his eyes.

"Thomas! Are you all right? Can you tell me where you are hurt?"

"I'm sorry, ma'am," he said hoarsely, "it should be me taking care of you, by rights. But my back seems hurt, like, and I don't think I can get up."

"Oh! Horrors," gabbled Isabella. "Catherine, what shall we do? We cannot remain here, and we cannot ride. And night is coming on. No one knows we are here, no one will come for us!"

"We must think what to do," said Catherine, to gain a little time. "Thomas, what do you advise? How far are we from Northanger?"

"Matter of four miles, thereabouts, now, ma'am," answered the old coachman, his eyes shut in pain. "There's a lantern by my seat – and a flint to light it. You might take that, and follow the road."

"Does it lead directly to Northanger?"

"That it does. If you could go and seek help-"

"I hate to leave you here. Is there any water?"

"Yes, a pouch."

"We will leave it with you. I wish there was something I could do for your pain."

"Bottle of spirits in the box – leave that with me too, if you would be so good," he said faintly.

She brought him the water, the spirits, and a blanket and left him to rest as comfortably as possible, promising to return with help as fast as might be.

"Is there any thing we can do for the horse?"

"No. I hope he can be splinted, but I can't tell from here. The best thing is to get some of the men from Northanger, right quick."

"We will." Then she looked at Isabella, who was sitting in the road, and starting to cry.

"Isabella! You must come with me. I do not want to walk alone to Northanger, and we will be safer together. Come. You can walk, cannot you?"

"I don't know. I don't want to."

"Nobody wants to," said Catherine through clenched teeth, "but we must. Come, the faster we walk, the sooner we will be there."

"It is a good thing you gave me new shoes," Isabella admitted.

There was no walking fast through the dark forest, however, and before long full darkness had fallen with only a gleam of moonlight above the trees. The girls trembled at every sound, every call of an owl, every cry of a wild dog, sure that the Gytrash, if such it was, would appear round the next bend.

"That creature would tear us to pieces," faltered Isabella. "Oh, where is it?"

"Nowhere near now. It went crashing off in the opposite direction after it overturned us, you know, and must be miles away by now. I wonder what it was."

"Something inhuman," shuddered Isabella, "a ghost or a demon. Oh! This terrible ancient forest, is full of strange things, I am sure!"

"Do stop talking like that, Isabella. I am only afraid if it comes back and menaces poor Thomas. Well, let us press on."

"Now my shoe has fallen off. Oh, Catherine, you are positively cruel. I cannot continue."

"You must, Isabella, for I am going on, and you do not wish to be left. I must get to Henry."

"Oh, he is all you think of. What about me?"

"The best thing for you," said Catherine uncompromisingly, "will be to get up and keep walking. Look – here is a stick. Take it and lean on it. That will help you."

"You must support me, Catherine, my ankle has been turned."

Isabella's complaints did not cease, and Catherine was hard put to reassure and encourage her, but at length the trees grew fewer, the moon overhead gave more light, and they entered a clearing. Half a mile further, and the Abbey appeared on a rise, a little ahead, gleaming through the clouds.

Chapter Twenty One

As soon as possible they were in the house, and Catherine was in Henry's arms. "Oh, my Catherine! What can have happened? Are you safe? You have not been harmed?"

Sinking into a chair she told him breathlessly of the carriage's overturning, and the accident to horse and coachman. "I am perfectly well, Henry, but look to Isabella - she is badly shaken, and hysterical."

The housekeeper took the sobbing and complaining Isabella upstairs to be cleaned up and put to bed in a room of her own, with assurances that she need not see Captain Tilney nor any one else tonight. Henry meanwhile gave orders for a party of men to start back on the road toward the overturned carriage. They bore a litter for Thomas, and the veterinary surgeon was summoned to go and see to the horse.

Catherine by this time had made her own toilet preparations for bed, and Henry found her tired but calm, and more than ready for rest.

"My Catherine, you really are a heroine! But how much you must have gone through. You are quite, quite sure you are unhurt?"

"Yes, very sure; we had not that far to walk, I have often taken longer country walks, and there was nothing to frighten one. Sometimes I am glad I was a tom-boy as a child! I do believe that has given me the foundations of the hardiness I enjoy now."

"Thank God you are strong, Catherine," Henry said fervently. "And it is wonderful that you have turned out a woman not only of strength, but of positively exemplary steadiness of mind! I used to think you rather a creature of imagination, but in truth the qualities of sense and sensibility are most admirably blent in your character. Think how you have conquered any tendency to imaginary horrors, and have nothing of hysteria about you, like poor Isabella. I am thankful for that; yet your literary foibles were great fun while they lasted," he finished with an affectionate smile.

"If I have learned sense it is due to your influence," she replied seriously. "But oh, Henry, I don't at all mean to return to imaginary fancies, but what could that mad horse have been? Where could it have come from? Isabella thought it was a goblin, or a Gytrash, that she read about in some story."

"What colour was it?" asked Henry, thinking hard. "Was it black, with a white star on its forehead?"

"Why, yes, it was. Do you know the horse?"

"I can make a pretty good guess. It is a horse that John Thorpe borrowed to ride while he was here, that he mistreated so badly it ran away. We did not know what had become of it."

"Oh! I hope it can be found, poor thing!"

"We will have the men search the countryside tomorrow, after poor Thomas has been brought here and treated, and the surgeon sees what can be done for the cob horse. This was at the entrance to the forest?"

"Yes."

"Well, think of it no more tonight, Catherine. We are together, and I hope Miss Thorpe will settle down after all she has gone through, and be more comfortable tomorrow. You are quite certain you are well, and are suffering no physical effects from the ordeal?"

"No indeed," she reassured him again with a smile. "I feel the child kicking quite healthily now, as a matter of fact."

"Thank God," he said fervently. "I would never have forgiven myself. But it is a fine thing to know that one has a wife with such fortitude and presence of mind."

"Oh, no I had not; I only kept on walking toward Northanger."

"But you did what you had to do. You seem to be making a habit of it – and here I have the idea that I ought to be the one protecting you! A fine job I have been doing of that!"

"I feel safe, now I am with you," sighed Catherine, as they nestled into the large four-poster bed with gay Chinese lemon silk coverings. "But tell me, Henry, how is Frederick?"

"He is low, very low. The doctor says he may begin sinking soon. We must see what we can do about him and Isabella tomorrow; I do not think it right that they should spend another night under this roof together, without benefit of wedlock."

"I hope Isabella may be able to take some little time about seeing him. Indeed, I do not know if she can be brought to consent to matrimony."

"It is a question for another day, and the men will take care of matters in the forest tonight. Do not think of these things again, but try to rest."

For answer she turned to him and they took their comfort in each other.

The world looked different in the morning, with the sun streaming through the long windows, on the green fields and hedges, as Catherine stretched her aching legs, still sore from the forest walk despite her good night's rest. Henry was not there, but she arose and went and knocked at Isabella's door, finding her pale and exhausted looking but willing enough to come down to breakfast.

Breakfast foods lined the sideboard, breads, cheeses and meats, with a covered platter full of eggs. The girls made a good meal, and felt considerably better. Henry who had been up for some hours, entered, and his eyes lightened at the sight of his wife.

"There you are, Catherine. Are you full well this morning, my love? And did you pass a comfortable night, Miss Thorpe?"

"I am perfectly well, thank you Henry, and Isabella is better too. Have the men returned with poor Thomas?"

"They have, and the doctor is with him now. He hopes that his back is not broken, only a strain, and that a few days rest will put him right."

"Oh, thank Heaven! Thomas was very brave and sensible the whole time."

"Yes, he is a good man. And the cob has been splinted, and will be led here slowly, in stages. It is a simple break, and there is no need to destroy him."

"I am very glad."

"As to this other business – "Henry looked at Isabella. "Are you equal to an interview with Frederick, Miss Thorpe? You may like to discuss his condition with the doctor, first."

"Yes – no," she said, and then, "I'll see the doctor."

Dr. Lyford came in from the chamber where Thomas had been placed, and sat down beside Isabella, speaking earnestly.

"Captain Tilney will not last many more hours, I am afraid, Miss Thorpe," he told her. "He is sinking, but still lucid, so if you think it best to perform the marriage ceremony, Mr. Tilney, this would be a suitable time."

"Is he – is he still mad?" Isabella asked fearfully.

"It is hard to tell. He has not said much. His frame is weakening, but if he is willing to consent to the marriage act, I see no reason why he cannot make the vows, if Mr. Tilney will perform them."

"Catherine – will you come with me?" Isabella asked.

Catherine swallowed, and nodded. "Certainly, dear Isabella. Let us go in to see him now."

Frederick looked weak and white, lying in bed, but he opened his eyes and nodded to Isabella, with what might or might not have been a look of contrition. When told what was intended, he nodded again, and Isabella consented to do as Henry advised.

The simple ceremony was soon over, and Isabella was assured that she need not remain in the sickroom with her new husband, but that it might be better for her shattered spirits to take the air in the garden. She sat there most of the afternoon, in a white wicker chair, looking out at the formally planted rose gardens and breathing their scent, while Catherine and Henry walked the grounds, and discussed the practical matters of the place. The horse was brought in, and pronounced to be doing well; and Henry interviewed the recovering Thomas, who confirmed that the mad horse was the same ridden by John Thorpe.

"Blackerby always was a gentle enough steed, and I am sure that if he can be made comfortable in the stables here and decently treated, he will make a good recovery."

Henry concurred, and dinner was soon announced. The young Tilneys and Isabella sat down without much appetite to roast fowl with parsnips and carrots from the Northanger farm. Afterward, Henry and Catherine, tired from the busy day, retired, tactfully leaving Isabella to join her new husband as he lay in his chamber. She went docilely enough, gathering her things but making no comment about the change in her status, only saying that she did not know if she could sleep.

"That is the room where I stayed watching your father the night after he died," Catherine reminded Henry, with a shudder. "I feel for Isabella, having to spend the night there with Frederick."

"I don't want to say that she made her bed and must lie in it," said Henry, "but there was nothing else to be done but to bring about that marriage. Come, let us go to bed and hope for a restful night ourselves."

A restful night, however, fell to nobody under the roof of Northanger Abbey. Some little while after the church bells tolled three, Frederick awakened in his father's bed to find Isabella lying asleep beside him. Weak though he was he sat straight up.

"What the devil are you doing here?"

Isabella woke with a fright. "Frederick! I am your wife. You must remember we were married today."

He gave her a shove. "Damned if you are! I'm not letting Northanger Abbey fall to your possession!"

"You – you agreed to it," she faltered. "I thought you cared for me."

"Cared! Well, it's not too late to put an end to this. I'll not consummate this cursed union, and tell my man of business to proceed for an annulment in the morning. I can't conceive how I was talked into such absurdity. It was my cursed weakness. But I am in my better mind now."

"Frederick! You don't mean it!" She tried to make him lie down again.

"Take your hands off me, woman!" She had not thought he had any strength left in him, but in his rage he got out of bed, and reached for a paper knife that lay on a nearby table. It was sharp enough and as he brandished it, Isabella leaped out of bed.

"Frederick! What are you doing? You *are* mad!"

He advanced toward her. "Call me mad, do you? You'll get out of here, one way or another, I tell you."

She backed away from him, and went through the double doors out onto the terrace, under a black and starry sky. He came menacingly after her, with the weapon, and although ill, he was still a tall hulking man, and with his gleaming maddened eyes, a terrifying figure.

"No!" she screamed, as he reached her. She tried to climb over the balustrade, perhaps with the thought of jumping off the ornamental parapet, in her panic. They were only on the second storey, and it was grass below. But he forestalled her with a push, surprisingly strong, and over she went.

She never reached the ground. An ornamental iron paling below, meant to hold a family flag, punctured her as she fell, and she was impaled halfway down, like a porker on a skewer. She died almost instantly, with a howling shriek that rent the night air and woke the house.

Frederick looked down at her body, still twitching on the flagpole, the scarlet Tilney banner furling itself around her corpse. Whether maddened or grieved, no one ever knew, but he flung himself over the balcony after her, instantly breaking his neck against a rock.

Catherine sat up in bed, terrified at the sound of Isabella's death cry and a following crash. "What was that!"

"Stay there, my dear – I will go and see."

Servants were heard in the halls, men running, and more screams. Doors opened and shut, but Catherine quailed and remained hidden under the covers.

Henry came back half an hour later, with an ashen face.

"What ever has happened, Henry?"

"Catherine – I hardly know how to tell you. They are both dead. Gone."

"What! Who do you mean? Not – "

"Yes. Frederick and Isabella. Both."

"But what in God's name can have happened? Tell me at once!"

"As far as we can make out – some of the servants heard Frederick and Isabella engaged in an argument. I should not have thought he had the strength for it, but somehow they both got out onto the balcony. She has fallen – or been pushed – who can tell – over the balustrade. It was a fall to her death, for she was impaled on an iron paling below."

Catherine could hardly speak. "Pushed? By - him?"

"Directly after she fell, Frederick evidently followed her to the edge, and somehow threw himself off the balcony after her. That is all we know so far, but it is enough."

"It is – is it the curse?" Catherine gasped.

"There are no curses, my dear," Henry reminded her, but he did not sound very convinced of it himself.

Chapter Twenty Two

The second and third funerals at Northanger in less than a week were speedily held, the coroner agreeing that death by misadventure could be the only verdict; and the newly married husband and wife were taken to lie together in the cold and stately Northanger vault, beside his father the General.

As soon as this sad business was over, Henry would hear nothing against returning at once with Catherine to Woodston, taking the view that the shock she had received might be deleterious to her condition, and she had better be at home.

The man of business, Claiborne, who in recent weeks had changed from attending to General Tilney's affairs, to Captain Tilney's, and now was advising Henry, tried to urge the young Tilneys to remain at the Abbey, which was now in their possession, but Henry would not hear of it.

"It may be mine," he argued, "I cannot deny that, but I am not at all certain it is incumbent upon me to live here, at least not at present."

"But my dear Mr. Tilney, there are the farms, and the tenants, and the affairs of the neighbourhood to see to. Northanger needs a master."

"My wife has been through too much, Mr. Claiborne, and she is in a delicate state."

"I understand," nodded Mr. Claiborne, "I hope that the shock has not hurt her, and that she will do well."

"I hope as much; but you can see the necessity of returning home at once for the sake of her health. There we can consider the situation at Northanger at our leisure. You are my agent, and can act for me for the time being."

Catherine was only too happy to go home to Woodston again, and thought that of all of their homecomings, this was the one for which she was most thankful. Sarah greeted her with joyous relief, and after she had been briefly told of the terrible events at Northanger, she no more wished to allude to the subject again than her sister.

Henry took care however to solicit Sarah's opinion as to Catherine's looks, and was much relieved to find that he thought her unaltered. "I do not think she is the worse for her ordeal," Sarah said, "she is very healthy you know, only might we not, perhaps, to ask the Allens to come and see her, on their way home from Bath?"

"That's well thought of, Sarah. Yes, will you write and invite them?"

"I will, if you like. And – another thing. What about my mother? It is a long journey from Fullerton, to be sure, but after hearing this story, I know she will not be easy unless she comes to see Catherine for herself."

Henry acquiesced. The placid and sensible temperament of the Allens would make their presence soothing to Catherine, and what young heroine, in a delicate condition, could not be in want of her own mother.

"I only hope the coming child will not be damaged by these portents and terrors," Sarah voicing the thought that was in every one's mind.

Henry tried to reassure her, but he was not at all certain of the effect of such shock and tragedy as Catherine had witnessed, on a young mother in a state of expectation. Fortunately Catherine did not seem unduly shaken, but he would not be at ease himself until he saw her under the care and had the opinion of her own sensible and matter-of-fact mother, who was nothing if not an expert on such matters.

Mrs. Morland was shocked in her turn by the events at Northanger, but it was her business to nurse and to soothe Catherine, and she did so with all the earnest energy of a good mother.

"So you think she will do well, Mrs. Morland?" Henry asked anxiously.

"To be sure, I should hope she will. She is a fine strong healthy girl, and here is Sarah who is just such another, and together we will keep Catherine quiet and her brains from working."

"Perhaps not so much as that," said Henry, to whom non-working brains were a step too far.

"It might be well to let her talk," was Mr. Allen's opinion. "To unburthen her own mind may do her good, if she likes it; but we must not mention the subject until she does. What happened to Captain and Mrs. Tilney is a hard tale to hear, but I think on the whole Catherine will be the better for getting it all off her chest, don't you, Mrs. Allen?"

"What is that? Oh, to let Catherine talk? By all means, and perhaps I may have the chance to beg her not to order any more of that flowered cretonne material, as she was going to do. There are rolls of it in a trunk in my room, I have discovered, quite enough to cover two sofas and a hassock."

Catherine did spend several hours in recounting all the incidents that had befallen her at Northanger, and on her journey thither. At one time or another she related the whole to her mother and Mrs. Allen, and they sat shaking their heads, exclaiming and moralizing, while Sarah's eyes were round in horror.

"Only think! A Gytrash! I have never heard of such a thing," was what Mrs. Allen picked out of all the terrors of the narrative to remark upon.

"I do not think they are real, Mrs. Allen, only a legend. And this one turned out to be John Thorpe's horse," explained Sarah.

"Did you hear if the poor creature was ever found?" asked Catherine.

"The horse Blackerby? Yes," Henry assured her, and described how he had been found in a field five miles away, and brought back to Northanger where he was recovering health and spirits after his ill usage.

"Thomas is able to care for the animal," he added, "and it is doing them both good."

"Such a story. And now how can any body say they do not believe in curses?" asked Sarah. "Poor Isabella! How her soul can be at rest after that, I declare I cannot imagine."

"She has been lain to rest in consecrated ground, with the proper Christian service," said Henry calmly, "and I am sure her soul must be at peace. I wish the same for my brother, but I do not know how far he had time to prepare to meet his Maker."

"What a pity if the spirits he had been drinking ended by destroying his immortal soul," said Mrs. Allen, placidly stitching on a piece of white muslin. "Catherine, do you prefer pink trim or blue trim on this little dress?"

"I cannot tell, as we do not know whether the child will be boy or girl, ma'am," she replied.

"She is carrying high," observed her mother, "and whenever I do that, it is always a boy."

With suchlike observations and the conversation turning to such pleasant prospects, Catherine soon improved in spirits and cheerfulness, and was content to spend the waning days of summer in her garden, with the beloved faces around her.

Occasionally she would come out with a meditation about General Tilney's murder, the curse on Northanger, and the unhappy newlywed couple who had met such a terrible fate there; but the prosings of Mrs. Allen and her mother had a tendency to counteract and soothe thoughts of that sort, swiftly enough. They were so matter-of-fact even in their exclamations, that the gory and gruesome began to seem outlandish even to Catherine, and she gradually stopped talking about the events. Henry began to have hopes that she might soon be able to put them out of mind entirely.

After a fortnight at Woodston, the Allens and Mrs. Morland departed for their home, traveling together in the Allens' carriage, and in due course, they were heard from as safe and settled at Fullerton following their journey. Mrs. Morland wrote an account of all her children, especially James, who had returned home from Oxford, having been ordained, and was hoping for a living in the neighborhood of Fullerton. Mrs. Allen sent Catherine a piece of lace she had been working for the baby.

Catherine had more leisure to listen with an attentive mind to Sarah, who now took the opportunity to pour out her heart about her renewed fears for the hopelessness of her own love affair.

Sarah had shown some restraint in keeping silence on the subject so long, until her sister's own mind was at ease; but it was not a happy retrospective.

"The sad thing, Catherine, is that I do not know, and probably can never know, Mr. Speedwell's heart," she confided as the two sisters stitched away on baby linen, not lifting their eyes from their work, lest each embarrass the other. "His family is so proud, and I think that is the real difficulty. And now this terrible story of Frederick and Isabella will stir up all the family prejudice again."

"His father is a Baronet, is not he? Do you know if he is a sensible man?"

"Yes, that is his rank, and John – Mr. Speedwell, is the oldest son. Lawyer though he is, I believe he feels bound to do as his father wishes, which is very praiseworthy, even if it goes against me," she sighed. "I do not know his father at all."

"You did like Mr. Speedwell very much, did you not," said Catherine sympathetically.

Sarah kept her eyes carefully lowered. "I did. But I do not think he will ever think of me again, now."

"But surely there is hope that he might?"

Sarah set down her work despairingly. "Oh, Catherine, how can you talk so! You know how all of Bath was full of nothing else but Captain Tilney and his Harriette and his Isabella – they were a public scandal, and on such a stage. And now madness and death – How can a girl with connections to such a family, ever expect to be countenanced? I understood what it meant, when Mr. Speedwell took his leave, and I cannot now expect to ever see him come back."

"You had nothing to do with any of the stories about Frederick and the Tilneys," Catherine said indignantly.

"To be sure not. But I was known to belong to some of the family, and that was enough."

"Can you be sure that was it? Whatever might be said about the Tilneys, they always were rich, and of good reputation in their county. And you are the daughter of a respectable clergyman."

Sarah shook her head sadly. "Don't you remember, how they invented an excuse to hurry Mr. Speedwell out of town? It was to prevent a possible alliance. I am sure his father not liking waters was half invented to get him away, Catherine," she said, and added in a wail, "and he went – he went!"

Catherine caressed and tried to cheer her younger sister, but all the time feeling it was hopeless, and Sarah was right in her assessment that she must not count on ever seeing Mr. Speedwell again. Even the commonest of sense would readily show him the solid wisdom of his family's reluctance to see him marry into a family connected to the cursed and immoral Tilneys.

Chapter Twenty Three

After the harvest, the autumn rains set in, and Woodston began to seem rather shuttered off from the world. All was warmth and harmony within, however. Catherine's health continued strong, and as months passed, she and Henry became more than ever confirmed in their certainty that they never would cease to be charmed by one another as companions. Her sister, too, was increasingly acceptable company, with her obliging nature and home associations. She looked up to Catherine, was eager to learn from her, and to have her sympathy about the disappointment that preyed upon her heart. They had many comfortable talks and readings together, especially at times when Henry was attending to parish matters or occupied in writing his excellent sermons.

All went well; Catherine did not expect her confinement until after Christmas, and her mother had promised to return then to be with her.

Henry had sufficient time to think about what were his duties toward Northanger. He and Catherine both loved their country home and church, to them a little paradise; but it was becoming apparent to both that if Woodston had all the pleasures, and Northanger all the pains, it might be right that an attempt be made to alter the place so as to lessen its painful associations, and make it a house of good feeling and good works.

At breakfast one October morning, Henry mulled over a letter, and finally brought himself to reluctantly open his thoughts to Catherine.

"Catherine, I have here a letter from Mr. Claiborne, the agent," he said. "It seems the rains have caused some considerable depredations in those tumble-down cottages the far side of Northanger – three roofs down, and the people in such distress."

"Oh, no, Henry! You will give orders for them to be repaired at once, will you not?"

"Certainly. But I am reminded that I have not been there these many weeks, and it is shameful to be so absentee a landlord as that. I really ought to ride over and see things for myself, but I dislike leaving you at such a time as this."

"Oh, surely that does not matter, and I can spare you for a short journey," Catherine tried to speak cheerfully, but Henry was not deceived.

"No; I am convinced that it would be wrong to put you through such anxiety. I know you would be thinking all the time of what happened the last time I went thither."

"It is true, I would not feel easy," Catherine admitted, "but in a practical way, it could not signify much for a night or two. And I shall have Sarah for company. Yes, do go, Henry, and see about those poor people."

"I really ought," he said hesitantly. "But oh, Catherine, what if there is a storm, and I am laid up there for a few days? What then?"

"I don't believe you will be," she said steadily, "and if you are, we will deal with it as it happens."

"Catherine, I honour you!" he cried. "No other woman would be so capable, so sensible, in not allowing her sad memories of that house to divert her from a proper decision."

"Well, I do have those memories," she confessed, "but they are best not thought of. I don't want to be fearful, and I believe I can be brave."

"I won't be away any longer than I can help," he promised.

He so hated to be away from his young wife at such a time, in fact, that he spent only one night away from Northanger, and came riding back at full pelt almost before she had begun to wonder when to expect him.

Barely had she come down from her heights of happiness and relief, and the enjoyments of his close embrace as she was seated upon his knees, when she started to realize that Henry was talking seriously – and that although he had come back from Northanger Abbey with such haste, he had been forming an idea of proposing that they take up residence therein.

"You don't mean it, Henry? To actually live at Northanger Abbey? Oh, no, surely not!"

"I think we ought to consider if it can be done. After all, I have inherited the place, and have a responsibility toward it, that much is clear. Northanger will go to ruin for want of a master."

Catherine was dismayed. "But you have your duties here, too, at Woodston parish. Surely the agent can run the business of Northanger, and you can visit as often as may be."

"As a temporary measure, yes. But Northanger deserves more than that. It is a large estate, and needs a very great deal of attention."

"Oh, Henry, you know we both loathe the very name of the place. Could you not sell it – or rent it to a good tenant? We are so happy here."

"We might rent it, perhaps, only there are things that must be done first, in all conscience. The church and graveyard must be properly re-consecrated."

"Do you mean, to dispel the curse the monks left on that unlucky place?"

"No; but the place has been given over to, shall we call it secular usage, by my father and brother," he said with a curl of his mouth. "If something is not done, Northanger Abbey will always carry a stigma, have a heavy cloud hanging over it. As a clergyman, I cannot help believing that it needs a kind of purification."

"It is all too true," said Catherine sadly.

"If the place is properly blessed, and if we live there in a peaceful and honorable way, while carrying out what repairs and improvements ought to be undertaken, I believe that our good work will go a long way."

Catherine did not look entirely convinced.

"Don't you see, we can make it the lovely historical home it ought to be, with peaceful associations. Then we can decide what course we want to take: to return to Woodston and find a tenant for the Abbey, or continue to live and raise our family in the family estate. The living of Woodston might then perhaps be given to your brother James, who would be a most suitable candidate."

Catherine promised to think over the plan, and only conditioned for not leaving Woodston until after their child was born, to which Henry replied that he would never think of anything else.

Their baby son, another Henry, was safely born just when he might be looked for, a few weeks after Christmas. Mrs. Morland came from Fullerton in time for Catherine's lying-in, and delighted in her first grandchild, though she was glad to return to her own household after a comparatively short visit of a few weeks. In truth, Catherine was not in need of much instruction about baby-tending, as she had been not only playfellow but almost second mother to her large family of younger brothers and sisters.

As the days grew cold outside, Catherine looked out the long windows of her pretty sitting-room at a snowy world instead of a green garden, but there could be few happier women in England than Mrs. Tilney, sitting by her fire with her baby on her knee.

It was decided that the family would move to Northanger Abbey with the coming of the spring weather, and Catherine was grown accustomed to the idea.

During these cold weeks, there was only one visitor who came to Woodston, and he was not a particularly welcome one. It was John Thorpe who came riding up in a rented gig, to be welcomed by the family with no feeling of pleasure.

Henry and Catherine gave him their condolences about the loss of his sister, as civilly as possible, but Thorpe seemed barely to be listening, or to care what they were talking about.

"Oh, Isabella – to be sure, that was so very shocking. Curses are terrible things. I am sorry she ever met that Captain Tilney, they are a devilishly bad family."

"You are speaking of my brother," Henry reminded him, with uplifted eyebrows.

"Yes, yes, but he is no loss is he, to say the truth? A bounder, was he not, with the temper of his father, and stingy into the bargain. Why, when I visited at Northanger Abbey last, he would barely let me take out any of his horses, and gave me just the crookedest, lamest old mare."

"If you have come all this way to complain about my late brother," said Henry with displeasure, "I wonder you have come at all."

"Aye, wondering is all very well, but I tell you I have a reason."

"And what is that?" asked Catherine, since no one else would.

"Why, it is just to talk to this young lady. Yes, you, my dear Miss Sarah," he said, leaning in toward Sarah with a soft smile which was grotesque on his broad face.

"Me! What can you mean, sir? Pray be brief – I am on my way to exercise the dogs and have no patience for conversation."

"Dogs! I have the finest hand in England in dealing with dogs. Let me walk with you, and if they misbehave I'll whip them to within an inch of their lives."

"Mr. Thorpe, kindly cease this kind of talking, it is despicable!" burst out the outraged Sarah.

"Oh, la, I can do sweeter talk well enough. Just you listen. I will even get down on my knees." And he followed actions to the words, and heavily got down off the sofa and onto one thick knee. From his pocket he withdrew a ring.

"Do you see that? It is a ring. My mother's own wedding ring. She does not need it any longer, my father being dead, so I coaxed her to give it to me, that I might offer it to the girl I love."

"Then I wonder why you show it here, sir," she said with disdain.

"Why, you are the girl, of course. You can't pretend that you do not know that I have been thinking of nothing but you all these long dreary winter months, Miss Sarah."

"I assure you I had no such idea, and have no pleasure in the thought, Mr. Thorpe."

"Well, well, I am perfectly serious. I know your father will not give you more than three thousand pounds, which is all he offered when your brother was to marry my sister; but perhaps it will be a bit more now, as he got Catherine off his hands without having to pay a penny, what with her marrying a rich man."

"I do not like this sort of talk, Mr. Thorpe, and beg to hear no more."

"Only let me finish. I am perfectly disinterested – I do not want your money, but am in love entirely and desire your hand. You are every bit as pretty as Catherine, I am convinced. I will take a little house near Fullerton, and am sure your father can help me to some income in the neighborhood around there, for your sake. We would be as happy as your sister and Mr. Tilney, whose married happiness you have been studying all winter, I perceive."

Sarah rose indignantly. "I would not marry you, Mr. Thorpe," she said with spirit, "if you were the last man in the world, and to prevent you from repeating your proposals I will now withdraw. I am sorry to disappoint you, but I hope to find you gone when I return. Good morning to you."

She walked out of the room, closing the door smartly, but even so it took the best part of an hour for Catherine and Henry to persuade John Thorpe that she really was sincere and his suit hopeless. Annoyed, because three thousand pounds would have been most convenient to clear his gambling debts, Thorpe at length ceased his remonstrances, and returned to Bath in his rented conveyance, and in a dudgeon.

When he had gone, Catherine expressed to Sarah her regret that her first proposal had been such a one.

"O, it does not signify," said Sarah, "I never would have accepted."

"Certainly not. And his behavior is just what it was to me in Bath, before I was married."

"No, did he propose to you too?"

"He certainly means to have one of you Morland girls," Henry observed, rising to go into his study.

"We had better warn the others," said Sarah. "What if Mary or Susan were taken unawares?"

"They would be perfectly safe. My father would never give permission," Catherine assured her.

Chapter Twenty Four

In the springtime, the work of restoration and purification began at Northanger, and it was a happier time than Catherine had expected. Henry was occupied all day long, with builders and farms, tenants and cottagers. Visiting churchmen came to confer about the re-sanctification of the church, and the county people paid visits of inspection, or at least, curiosity.

Henry would not neglect Catherine for business, however, and leaving the baby with Sarah and the servants, they would walk together every fine morning, enjoying the snowdrops and the bluebell woods, and spying the first crocuses, while they exchanged news and discussed the work that was going on and was of such vital importance to their lives.

This peaceful time was interrupted, however, by a jolting discovery that amounted to a recurrence of the disturbing and dark times now considered to have been consigned to the past history of Northanger

Abbey. Workmen clearing out the labyrinth of underground and cellar passages in the oldest part of the building, came across two skeletons, of a man and a woman, neither of them very long deceased. In the ensuing hubbub, Dr. Lyford and Mr. Carter were summoned, as they were growing to expect to be at all tragic events at Northanger; and the local magistrate and his subordinates were hard on their heels.

Catherine was not left long in suspense about these discoveries. After Henry was closeted with the workmen and visitors for an afternoon, he went to find his wife, who had considerately gone to her chamber with the baby, so as to be well out of the way of whatever was befalling Northanger now.

"Catherine, you have seen all the comings and goings today, and I must tell you what it is about. They have found the body of that Frenchman."

She looked up, startled. "No! But how can that be, Henry? We thought he was long gone, away from here."

"That is what Frederick thought, I know, but it was not so. Evidently he doubled back in some way and returned to Northanger in stealth. Then he met with some accident in the cellars – no one is sure yet what happened exactly."

"How horrible!" She thought a moment. "There is no information, I suppose, no evidence, that he really did murder your – General Tilney?"

"No, and I don't know if such proof will ever be found. All that is certain is that the man did return, and somehow died in the underground passage."

"I never knew about that passage. Was it made by the monks?"

"Yes, it is very ancient, and is walled up, so there is no easy access. We have no way of knowing, and probably never will have, whether M. Blaine came back in search of Harriette, as she thought, or for some French spy secrets, as I suspect. Whatever the case, he must have blundered into the underground entrance, and fallen into it only to his own peril and ruin."

Catherine shuddered. "To think he was here, after the General died, and when Frederick was master of the house. Do you think Frederick knew?"

Henry shrugged. "Who can tell? My brother kept his own counsel. You never knew what his motives were." He stopped. "Not to speak ill, but think how oddly he behaved after my father's death, how he tore all over the countryside hunting for this man, when there was no reason to think he could ever be found. But I now perceive that Frederick seemed halfway demented in those days, and did all manner of odd things. I remember in those few days he was at home in between his two hunting excursions for the Frenchman, he gave some very strange orders."

"Did he? Of what sort?"

"Oh, he railed against my father's extravagance, and sacked a good many people – the head gardener and some of his men, several coachmen, and a host of what he called supernumerary kitchen servants, mostly women. It was a shame, but there was no arguing with him, and I still don't know what has become of all those people. I should have made inquiries long before this; it was very remiss of me. Some of the servants may have been in distress, and in need of help. And they are our own village people, from time out of mind."

"Do not fault yourself, Henry, you had so much to think of during those terrible months."

"That is no excuse. I should have given proper thought. But, Catherine," he hesitated. "There is more than that."

"More than finding the French visitor who may have been responsible for your father's death? What on earth can you mean, Henry? Really you make me think of my first visit to Northanger, when you regaled me about the housekeeper Dorothy, and all that would menace me, and I believed every word!"

"It is no joke now, dear Catherine, I am afraid. I must tell you that they have found a second body."

"Not really!" Catherine sank back in her seat, her hand at her heart. "But who – what can it be?"

"That question cannot yet be answered, but we do know that the body is that of a woman."

Their eyes met, and Catherine's were dilated in horror. "A woman! The Frenchman had an accomplice, then? A partner perhaps? Another girl like Harriette?"

"No, I gather not. The workmen reported that she was an old woman, very pale as if she had not seen sunlight in many years, and she was all dressed in grey. She must have been your Grey Lady."

"She was killed in the accident?"

"I do not believe so. She was in another part of the corridor, a chamber where apparently she lived; and horrifyingly enough, it seems as if she must have perished for want of, of food, or water."

His voice sank, and he buried his head in his hands.

"My Grey Lady," said Catherine wonderingly. "Do you mean to say that she was – walled up in that place?"

"I fear so. Oh, Catherine, I thought we could purify this house, start again, begin a happier story here; but there seems no end to the true horrors of Northanger, does there? It seems an hopeless task."

"You, a clergyman, a Man of God, of all people, must never give up making the world better, and I will help," she reminded him, with spirit.

He took her hand and smiled at her. "My Catherine, how good you are, how always right. I used to think myself so clever, but I do perceive that you are the one of us with the very best sort of sense, and that is wisdom."

"I am not wise enough," she said humbly, "and you have been affected far more than I have by the tragedies here, as Northanger was your home. What we must do, I think, is to face things squarely, and together."

"That is right. Come, Catherine, I will keep nothing hidden. We will go together to see what more may have been discovered, or conjectured, if any thing."

The young Tilneys were calm as they entered the drawing-room together, where those in authority were finishing their discussion with the workmen.

"Ah, here you are, Tilney," said the agent, Claiborne, whose usually genial expression was more sober than Henry had ever yet seen. "I am afraid you must be informed about a fresh revelation, and very sad it is. Who can best tell him?" He looked around the room, but all were silent.

"Tell me what?" asked Henry. "Do not wait, Claiborne, out with it. What have you found now?"

The agent looked at the doctor. "You have known the family longest, Lyford," was all he said.

The doctor cleared his throat. "Mr. Tilney, it grieves me to tell you this. But one of the workmen – an older man, who has worked on the estate for many years – has said that he believes he knows who was the woman found in the tunnels."

"Well? And who was she?"

"We very much fear, Mr. Tilney, that she was your mother."

Chapter Twenty Five

The terrible news about Mrs. Tilney was not something Henry could recover from in haste. It was a very great shock. His mother, whose decline and death he had witnessed as a young man, ten years ago – or thought he had - how was it possible that she could have survived? He had seen her lying waxen and still, with his own eyes, as had Frederick. Eleanor had been from home, at school, and only arrived to see the already closed coffin.

Now Eleanor came as swiftly as the fastest horses could bring her and her husband, not four and twenty hours since the most shocking of all discoveries. Henry had been badly shaken by having to identify the body and confirm that it was, indeed, Mrs. Tilney, but the arrival of his sister did something toward a beginning of restoring his composure. Considerate of what he knew would be her feelings, he collected himself enough to receive Eleanor with a warm reassuring embrace and lead her to a seat in the garden, where he regarded her with anxious compassion. Charles and Catherine watched the brother and sister with concern of their own.

Eleanor was the first to find her voice. "Was it really – our mother?" she asked. "How could this possibly be? Surely it is a mistake?"

"We still don't altogether know what happened," he told her. "But the lady is indeed our dear mother. Dr. Lyford, and Mr. Carter, and I, all concur that she did not die in what we thought was her last illness."

"But you saw her then, Henry?" asked Eleanor, bewildered. "And Frederick saw her. You both told me that she was gone."

"She was still and white when I saw her," said Henry with difficulty, "and I did not question what my father told me. I was only permitted to glimpse her from the doorway, for a brief moment; and I was very greatly affected. I remember I could hardly bear to look."

"And I too believed what I was told," reflected Eleanor. "But the doctors – they surely certified her death?"

"I had not come into attendance upon the family yet, you remember," said Dr. Lyford, "but I never heard of any thing strange or out of the way about it. There was no talk."

"It was my predecessor who certified the death," added Mr. Carter. "It might be a matter of inquiry to unearth Mrs. Tilney's tomb, and see who – or what – or if any thing is buried there."

"However it was managed, and why, it is a fact that this woman did survive, and was kept walled up in a secret compartment in the catacombs, for an entire decade," concluded the doctor.

"My mother! Oh, and all the time we thought her gone, I might have had the indescribable happiness of seeing her," said Eleanor, in tears.

Henry turned away and could not look at his sister.

"And I," murmured Catherine, "might have known her."

"Mr. Carter," said Eleanor presently, "tell me, if you can, what were her quarters like? Do you believe she suffered very much in them?"

"You can see the room," said the doctor, but Eleanor only shuddered. "No, no."

"It is a pleasant enough chamber, with a water-closet, lamps, and books. She might have been comfortable in body, though I have no doubt that if she had been sane during those years, she must have missed her children grievously, and perhaps tried to escape."

"But why was she kept in captivity? And why? Did my father do it?" asked Eleanor, bewildered.

"He must have done it," Henry concluded reluctantly, turning around to face her. "Who else? She had unquestionably been very ill; perhaps he thought it was the action of the curse. Perhaps that was why he kept her confined, in order to keep her safe. No one will ever know, now."

"But that is madness indeed," exclaimed Catherine. "What could he hope to gain by such behavior, keeping her a prisoner?"

"There is reason to believe that he did think her a madwoman," the doctor replied, trying to speak carefully. "Her health must have been very frail, after such an illness, with her weakness the result of all she endured from him over so many years. By all accounts it was a most severe bilious fever, which must have left her weak, and in pain. We found medicines there, that made it appear that she was given sedatives which would have kept her quiet, and also prevented her from trying to escape. They are medicines such as are given to the mad."

"How horrible," murmured Catherine, while Eleanor was crying openly, and her husband trying to comfort her.

"Catherine, how extraordinary that you always suspected something like this, and that you should have been proved right," Henry could not help saying.

"I only read about such things in novels," she answered, bewildered, "and was goose enough to think they might occur in real life."

"On the contrary," Henry replied, "it now appears that your suppositions showed a mind of some considerable genius."

"No," protested Catherine, "Now I see that it was not that I really believed my readings, but that I suspected General Tilney's nature. You were used to it, but he was a sort of person who was quite new to me."

"I can easily believe that," said Charles, looking at his wife with pity. "When I think of what Eleanor's life was with him…"

Eleanor wiped her tears. "Don't think of it, Charles," she urged, "it is over, and let us only think how happy we are together now."

"It took little imagination to realize that perhaps General Tilney had been cruel - had not been kind to your poor mother."

"Yes. You were judging his character rather than his actions. And now his actions have proved him to be uncannily like what you thought him. In looking back – to think that a man of his intellect and achievements could have fallen under the rhodomontade of a John Thorpe, and cast you out of his house as a result – why, Catherine, he might almost have been suffering from derangement himself."

"Softening of the brain, perhaps," contributed the doctor.

"And you and I, Henry, never thought of such a thing."

"No, Eleanor. We were too close, and had been bullied every day for years; we were his victims almost as much as our mother. I blame myself for not protecting you better, however. You were too often left to his tender mercies. I always hated to leave you alone with him."

"Do not quarrel for the honors of a share of the guilt," Dr. Lyford advised. "It is often so when a person begins to show signs of derangement, and

General Tilney had been of very difficult character for as long as you knew him. You did not make him the way he was, and must not take blame."

"And we must remember," Catherine mentioned, "he kept your mother living. He did not murder her; nor was she starved, was she? How did she eat, how was food and water provided?"

"I think we can answer that," said Claiborne. "The gardener's men were dismissed by Frederick, but one Tom White, a laborer, still lives in a cottage on the estate with his old grandmother. He is waiting to tell his story. Let us bring him in now, shall we."

White, a short but sinewy young man, had little education, and almost all he knew had to do with what his task had been, the digging of vegetables, and he was frightened at being summoned to speak to the gentlefolk. Henry gently questioned him, however, and drew out his recollections that the head gardener, Wantage, often was called in to private closetings with General Tilney, and given special instructions.

"He was to grow certain food," White told them, "nothing fancy, a few swedes and potatoes and corn and such like, kept apart special."

"But where did he grow them?"

"Why, in the General's pine-apple glasshouse."

"And no one saw them there, or asked about them?"

"Law, no. It was as much as your place was worth, to set foot in that there glass house. Only Wantage did that. None of us was allowed."

"And you think he grew food for her there?" Henry asked incredulously.

"It seems likely to have been so," concluded Dr. Lyford. "I deduce that Wantage must have been charged to supply Mrs. Tilney with her meals. He could deliver them to her chamber from the garden door, quite easily."

"And his cottage was right hard by," pointed out White.

"He could cook there?"

"Certain sure."

"Wantage the gardener – I remember him," said Catherine in some surprise. "I always liked him, and used to stop and talk to him about his plants. He would cut posies for me."

"Yes, so he did," said Eleanor. "He once asked me about the visiting young lady, and if Mr. Henry was not very taken with her. Catherine, do you know – I wonder if it was he who left that note on your door?"

Catherine's eyes dilated. "Why, it might have been! He must have meant it as a warning!"

"To keep you from marrying into the family, and suffering a fate like that of my poor mother, as he may have feared," Eleanor concluded.

"Wantage's duties must have become increasingly painful for him to carry out, as her strength declined," the doctor considered. "And General Tilney died too suddenly, it is evident, to pass on to any body the secret of his wife's survival, and her need for care."

Claiborne agreed. "And don't you recall, after the General's death, almost Frederick's first act as master of Northanger was to immediately sack the gardener? I asked him why he wanted this done, and he said he considered his father's gardening his most expensive and excessive hobby horse. He would spend no more on it, and the head gardener was the first to go, to be followed by his minions, as Frederick put it."

"Yes, Frederick did always did detest that greenhouse," said Henry, "but I never realized to what extent. It seemed to represent every thing he hated about his father."

"He never knew that his action in turning away Wantage, was his own poor mother's death sentence," said the coroner.

"Good God," Henry exclaimed. "I cannot think of it. But what became of Wantage?"

"He suffered a paralytic stroke within days of the General's death, and was taken to his daughter's house, in Gloucester," said the doctor. "When I saw him, he was laid up, unable to speak, but he may have improved, and retain understanding enough to confirm or deny this whole story."

"It will be looked into," said the coroner, "and Mrs. Tilney's tomb opened."

"It is incredible," said Henry, "I can hardly take this all in. To think we might have seen, might have helped our mother, Eleanor."

"It is too terrible to contemplate," she whispered, and swayed, as if she might faint.

She was soon revived, with wine and water, and taken up to bed by her husband and Catherine.

"I don't know how Eleanor will ever recover from this," Henry said, "she loved her mother so very dearly, and was so desolate after she was gone."

"It falls hard upon you too, my boy," the doctor said gravely.

"It is, but I have my Catherine, and our baby, and our happy life at Woodston. I never can forget my mother's tragedy, but remember her gentle soul, and know how happy she would have been if she could have seen our happiness. To think she could have! She was still alive, all that time. Oh, how I wish we could have spoken."

"Though she is dead, she speaketh," the doctor intoned soberly. "Mr. Tilney, I did not want to show you this whilst your sister was present, for fear she might be overset. But I will show you now, and you can decide for yourself when to tell her about this finding. This – document was in your poor mother's chamber, and in her hand."

He drew from his pocket a small scrolled parchment, scratched on in faint ink.

"That is my mother's writing," breathed Henry.

"Would you read it aloud, Mrs. Tilney?" asked the doctor.

Catherine took the parchment with some reluctance, remembering the others she had read in the General's room.

"Yes, go ahead, Catherine," Henry encouraged her.

"My dearest children,"

Catherine read.

> "How it breaks my heart to see you at Northanger, and I not able to approach you, or speak to you. Yet I have seen you, time and again. You do not know how often I have glimpsed you, followed you, peered in at you, in my sadness and my love. Frederick, you have grown to be a fine man; I hope your character is as stalwart as your figure, and that you will prove to be a benevolent Master of Northanger Abbey, and an honour to your country. Henry, my sweet son, I have been made so happy to know that you have become a man of God, and I rejoice in your wedding to your Catherine, which your father has told me of. I wish you both joy for ever, and I know you will treasure for my sake the little piece of tapestry I worked for your bride."

Catherine looked up. "She did – the Grey Lady left me a piece of stitchery with a kind message embroidered into it. I have kept it, and we will treasure it always. Now let me go on."

> "And Eleanor, my darling girl – you are all I ever hoped you would become, and it is the greatest heartbreak of all that I could not complete my

mission of being a mother to you, and guide you to womanhood.

When, someday, you read this, you will know that your father has kept me shut up in these dismal quarters for at least a decade; he thinks me mad, and so I suppose I am in some ways; but he is the one who is not only mad but cruel. When I fell ill he conceived that the curse of Northanger had fallen upon me, and he sequestered me away in his mad solicitude, to keep me safe. He would sit with me now and then, not deigning to speak often, and I was hard put to it to conceal that the sight of him was so much worse than entire solitude would have been. My only other visitor was the gardener, dear old Wantage, who looked after my needs, and to whom I have much reason to be grateful.

I dared never try to speak to you, or break the secret of my confinement, for your father threatened to murder you all, and certainly myself, if I dared; and as I have grown weaker and frailer over these years, I accepted my lot, as the punishment of God for marrying such a man; and I would do nothing to endanger you. It was enough to know, from my brief glimpses of your faces, that you were well, and you were happy.

Wantage has told me of your father's death, and I hope to be soon released from here, and know the great joy of being reunited with you; but I have a foreboding, for he has not been here in some days, and I grow faint from lack of nourishment. I confess that I fear Frederick may have interfered in some way, but I will wait a little longer; in any case I am all but certain that my own death is nearly upon me.

All that remains, my dearest children, is for me to tell you how much I love you, and always have, and always will. God's blessing upon you, and your children, forever more.

Your loving mother.

E. Tilney"

There was a silence, which Charles interrupted by coming down stairs to report that Eleanor was quiet, and would soon be asleep. "I think she will be better in the morning," he said to the anxious Henry. "She is such a sensible woman, you know, and will endeavor to think of other things; and I hope that all will soon be as if this never was."

"I don't know if that is possible quite yet," Henry told him. "We have more to tell you, Charles, and you must help us to judge how much should be made known to my sister. A letter has been found from my mother, to her children."

"No! Can it be?"

"Read it yourself." And Henry proferred the parchment.

After reading the sad missive, Charles looked up. "Knowing Eleanor's tenderness, I have great fears," he said, "but her love of her mother was so deep, and her heart so badly broken by her loss, that I could not in all conscience keep this message from her. You do not recommend such a thing?"

"I do not at all know," said Henry. "I have hardly taken it in myself. My mother! Speaking to us, after so long. And now her voice is silenced. It breaks one's heart, for her, even more than for us."

"It does, Henry," Catherine said softly, "but I am sure that, however painful, Eleanor ought to know of her mother's last loving message to her. She will cherish it for ever."

"Yes, I will tell her of it, gently," Charles decided. "And then, afterwards, I will endeavor to help Eleanor, as Catherine will help you, Henry."

"You will be her best consolation," said Henry gratefully, "as Catherine is mine."

"And once the message has been digested, I think, I believe, that Eleanor will not want to remain in this place for long, but to go home to Eastham House, and to our happy life there."

"I am sure you are right," said Henry ruefully. "I can hardly bear the thought of Northanger Abbey myself."

Chapter Twenty Six

The purification of Northanger Abbey was soon completed, by a convocation of churchmen; but it made surprisingly little difference to the feelings of Henry and Catherine. Mrs. Tilney's tomb was opened, and created a sensation by proving to be empty. Eleanor cried much over her letter and the tapestry, but as Catherine had thought, she was infinitely thankful to have the precious words of her mother whom she had loved and missed so much, and was soon resigned to a death that she had long ago accepted.

The Christian burial of poor Mrs. Tilney could therefore take place, and did bring some peace and serenity to the hearts of those who mourned her. The body of the Frenchman, as a murderer, could not be buried in consecrated ground, and he was carried to a potter's field where he might lie forgotten.

Eleanor and Charles departed for their home immediately after Mrs. Tilney's second burial; and Henry redoubled his efforts to complete all necessary business, promising Catherine that they need not remain at Northanger very much longer, after surveying what was still to be done.

There was however still considerable work in hand, cottages to be renewed, the spring planting to be got underway, and also the important business of tracing the former, scattered workers. The final decision of what would be their permanent abode was not yet taken, but they decided to send for Sarah, who had been left to herself too long at Woodston. She was very glad to come, and enjoyed watching the progress of the work on Northanger, and playing with baby Henry.

Most of the others who arrived at Northanger at that period were principally tradesmen and workmen, for the gardens were projected to be kept up so as to provide food for the tenants, thus enabling them to help themselves; and there was still much building and renewing work to accomplish.

One visitor however came in a gentleman's carriage, as Catherine, sitting with Sarah in the morning room enjoying the early sunshine, and looking out at the long drive, was the first to see.

"I wonder who it can be, I do not know the carriage," she said. "Another of the county neighbors perhaps, to see how the building is doing, and then going away to gossip about it."

Sarah leaned forward and could not conceal her startled exclamation.

"Why, what is it, Sarah?"

"It is Mr. Speedwell," was all that Sarah replied, looking down at her sewing again.

Catherine now recognized her sister's acquaintance, and as he entered the house she quickly saw in him the same handsome, personable, well spoken young man as he used to be, and with the same true gentility in his considerate mode of address. She had always liked him, and from what she could see of Sarah's blushing cheek, turned away studiedly, Sarah was being made completely happy by this visit.

Feeling herself a matron almost middle-aged by the sight of her sister, Catherine knew her duty, as well as her own mother had when Henry Tilney had come a-courting to Fullerton, only two years since. She suggested that Sarah show Mr. Speedwell the gardens, while she attended to her child; and he did not have to be asked twice.

Certain it is that when the young couple returned to the house for tea with Catherine, they were indeed an affianced pair; and when Henry returned from a meeting with the farm manager, he was welcomed into the great secret as rapidly as possible.

After congratulations had been bestowed on them, Sarah began to question her lover. "But how could you know where to find me?" she wanted to know. "Did you really come all the way here for that?"

"I did indeed," he insisted. "I knew when I was forced to leave Bath that I cared for you; but I could not be certain if the feeling was returned. I hated to leave when your family was in such trouble, but I did not like to intrude on what must have been your grief and discomfiture. Then, too, my father was distressed; and I thought it best to obey him."

"We are glad you are here, Mr. Speedwell," Henry assured him heartily, "and you find us not in grief any longer, but in great happiness."

"So my scandalous connections did not deter you after all?" Sarah was curious to know.

"Hardly that! I told my father that after bending to his will and enduring months of thought and regret as a consequence, I was fully convinced of my mistake, and he could not disagree with a mind so made up as mine was. I went to Bath to find out if there was any news of you, for if you were married or about to be married I would be likely hear it there."

"Yes, the Tilney family was so widely spoken of, the gossips of the town would certainly latch onto such a detail," said Catherine.

"Now, Mrs. Tilney, you know how it is, there is always something new going on in Bath, and so many scandals and shocking instances of elopements and quarrels are always occurring, even since our departure. All the happenings at Northanger Abbey are, if you will forgive me, now yesterday's news."

"We always think our own story the most important," Henry observed. "The name of Tilney is doubtless forgotten in Bath by this time, and I am very glad it should be so."

"Not quite forgotten," said Speedwell with a smile. "There is one who remembers it only too well."

"Who is that? The Allens are not there now, it is not their time for Bath."

"What about John Thorpe? Ah ha! I see I am right," laughed Henry.

"You are," said Speedwell. "I encountered him taking the waters – he has grown quite stout and is drinking the waters to reduce – and he expatiated at great length on Sarah's rejection of his suit. He was sure she threw him over for the sake of getting a man with a profession; a lawyer like myself, he said, was exactly what she wanted, and I had better make tracks and stay away from the craven creature for she hadn't a red cent to her name."

"He said that?" exclaimed Catherine, amazed.

"Oh yes. It was the first hint that gave me any real hope of obtaining Sarah's affections, and I lost no time in driving directly here, where Thorpe was sure I would find her, after more horrors that he announced had happened at Northanger Abbey."

"But they did not deter you?" asked Sarah, her eyes shining.

"No, my love. Here I am, you see, with my proposal, at your feet."

Sarah began to rush into his arms, only to stop with a gasp.

"But what is the matter, my dear?"

"Oh, I hate to owe my happiness to that odious John Thorpe!"

"That is no moral to draw from it, Sarah. You owe your happiness to my love and to your own, and nobody and nothing else."

"And we shall live in Bath?"

"Yes, that is where my practice is, and I shall take a very good house, large enough to entertain all your family when they come calling."

"You don't know how large my family is," she laughed.

"I am glad to see a happy event transpiring at Northanger Abbey," said Henry. "Perhaps it means that the curse is quite off the place now, Catherine!"

"I don't mind my proposal having taken place here one bit," Sarah said cheerfully. "The sooner the better, and I will always like old Northanger the better for the remembrance."

"That is very good of you," said Henry gratefully. "We must see that some happy memories are collected here, and this is a good beginning."

"And I don't believe in curses any way, Mr. Tilney. Do you, John? Surely not. You would not marry into a cursed family."

"No, I only see blessings, I must say," he replied. "What say you, Mrs. Tilney?"

"My wife is a firm and permanent convert to science and rationalism," said Henry, meeting Catherine's eyes with a twinkle in his own.

"Certainly," she assented, "you have had me read all about the Lunar Men, and Darwin, and Locke. Curses are but silly superstition, and knowing this has helped me put all the sad happenings here out of mind."

"They were not due to a monk's curse, but to a family's sadness, handed down through the misfortunes over several generations," said Henry seriously. "I believe that such unhappy events as early deaths and misfortunes, can warp and harm a young, growing person, and damage his character. Then he may inflict his own pain upon others around them, even upon his children. I believe that is the story of my father."

"Yes. And the way to combat that tendency to melancholy and passion, engendered by such early tragedy, is to live in such a way as to cause no pain to others, and to be kind and loving to our own children."

"That is a good philosophy," said Sarah, "and certainly one which we will follow, won't we, John?"

"To be sure we will," he agreed, taking hold of her hand. "I like that moral."

"So now do you believe Northanger is truly healed, Catherine? Would you like to remain here, in the seat of my patrimony? I will leave it up to you."

"Will you, Henry? We both love Woodston so, but should you like to stay at Northanger? I do believe you are right, and we could make it a beautiful home; and perhaps it is our duty to help others in the neighborhood, and do what good we can. Is that what you think?"

"I am willing to try, if you are. Your brother can live at Woodston, and we will visit often. I am convinced we do owe a duty to Northanger and its people, to repair the damage some of my forbears have caused. In doing our duty, however, we can make it a pleasure, as with every thing we do. And I know you really do not believe in curses any more, if you ever did."

"No," said Catherine, "though I must say that there are some things between heaven and earth, that cannot quite be explained."

About the Author

Diana Birchall worked for many years as a story analyst for Warner Bros. Studios, reading novels to see if they would make movies. Reading popular manuscripts went side by side with a lifetime of Jane Austen scholarship, and resulted in her writing Austenesque fiction both as homage and as close study of the secret of Jane Austen's style. She is the author of *Mrs. Darcy's Dilemma* and *Mrs. Elton in America*, as well as *In Defense of Mrs. Elton* and hundreds of short stories, many written for the Austen Variations website (http://austenvariations.com/). Her Austenesque comedy plays have been performed in many cities, with "You Are Passionate, Jane," a dialogue between Jane Austen and Charlotte Bronte in Heaven, being presented at Chawton House Library in England.

Diana has also written a scholarly biography of her grandmother, the first Asian American novelist, Onoto Watanna, and has lectured widely about her books at universities including Yale, Columbia, and NYU. Diana grew up in New York City, and now lives in Santa Monica, California, with her poet husband Peter and three cats, Pindar, Martial, and Catullus. Her son Paul is the Catalina Island Librarian.

Acknowledgments

Thanks to my son, Paul Birchall, my best editor and joke-provider, who is more than a little like Henry Tilney (in his mother's opinion!).

Thanks to Abigail Reynolds and all the Austen Variations group for their great help and encouragement.

And thanks to Dr. Oscar A. Estrada and the pulmonary team at UCLA Santa Monica Medical Center, who helped my husband Peter get well, so that he and I could be together and write again.

Printed in Great
Britain
by Amazon